Terrible Beauty

Molotov Betrothal: Book 1

Anna Zaires

♠ Mozaika Publications ♠

This is a work of fiction. Names, characters, places, and incidents are either the product of the author's imagination or are used fictitiously, and any resemblance to actual persons, living or dead, business establishments, events, or locales is purely coincidental.

Published by Mozaika Publications, an imprint of Mozaika LLC.
www.mozaikallc.com

Cover by Alex McLaughlin

Photography by Regina Wamba
www.reginawamba.com

e-ISBN: 978-1-63142-743-5
ISBN: 978-1-63142-744-2

Chapter 1

Present Day, Location Unknown

Cool lips brush my throbbing forehead, bringing with them a faint aroma of pine, ocean, and leather. "Shh... It's okay. You're okay. I just gave you something to ease your headache and make this easier."

The male voice is deep and dark, strangely familiar. The words are spoken in Russian. My fuzzy mind struggles to focus. Why Russian? I'm in America, aren't I? How do I know this voice? This scent?

I try to pry open my heavy lids, but they refuse to budge. Same goes for my hand when I attempt to lift it. Everything feels impossibly heavy, like my very bones are made of metal, my flesh of concrete. My head lolls to one side, my neck muscles unable to support its weight. It's as if I were a newborn. I try to speak, but an incoherent noise escapes my throat, blending with a distant roar that my ears can now discern.

Maybe I am a newborn. That would explain why

I'm so ridiculously helpless and can't make sense of anything.

"Here, lie down." Strong hands guide me onto some soft, flat surface. Well, most of me. My head ends up on something elevated and hard, yet comfortable. Not a pillow, too hard for that, but not a stone either. There isn't much give in the object, but there is some. It's oddly warm as well.

The object shifts slightly, and from the foggy recesses of my mind, the answer to the mystery emerges. *A lap.* My head is lying on someone's lap. A male someone, judging by the steely, thickly muscled thighs underneath my aching skull.

My pulse accelerates. Even with my thoughts sluggish and tangled, I know this isn't normal for me. I don't do laps or men. At least I haven't thus far in all of my twenty-five years.

Twenty-five. I grab on to that sliver of knowledge. I'm twenty-five, not a newborn. Encouraged, I sift through more of the tangled threads, seeking an answer to what's happening, but it eludes me, the recollections coming slowly, if at all.

Darkness. Fire. A nightmare demon coming to claim me.

Is that a memory or something I saw in a movie?

A needle biting deep into my neck. Unwelcome lassitude spreading through my body.

That last bit feels real. My mind might not be functioning, but my body knows the truth. It senses the threat. My heart rate intensifies as adrenaline saturates my veins. Yes. Yes, that's it. I can do it. With strength born of growing terror, I force open my leaden eyelids and look up into a pair of eyes darker than the night surrounding us. Eyes set in a cruelly handsome face that haunts my dreams and nightmares.

"Don't fight it, Alinyonok," Alexei Leonov murmurs. His dark voice holds both promise and threat as he gently threads his fingers through my hair, massaging away the throbbing tension in my skull. "You'll only make it harder on yourself."

The edges of his calluses catch on the tangles in my long hair, and he pulls his fingers out, only to curve his palm around my jaw. He has big hands, dangerous hands. Hands that have killed dozens today alone. The knowledge roils my stomach even as some knot of tension deep inside me unravels. For ten long years, I've dreaded this moment, and finally, it's here.

He's here.

He's come for me.

"Don't cry," my husband-to-be says softly, brushing away the wetness on my face with the rough edge of his thumb. "It won't help. You know that."

Yes, I do. Nothing and no one can help me now. I recognize that distant roar. It's the sound of a plane engine. We're in the air.

I close my eyes and let the hazy darkness take me.

Chapter 2

11 Years and 3 Months Earlier, Moscow

A tentative knock falls on my bedroom door. "Alina, are you in there? Come on, it's time for our lesson."

Yeah, fuck that. I pause the game I'm playing on the Wii and thumb up the volume on my iPod until "Get Low" by Lil' Jon & The East Side Boyz is blasting in my ears, drowning out the annoying voice of my tutor.

Muting the sound on the TV, I resume the game and guide Mario down the road, ignoring the continuous knocking. I don't know why I have to take English lessons all summer long when I've been studying at a boarding school in New Hampshire for the past three years. By now, my English is as good as any of my American classmates', my Russian accent nonexistent. Sure, my spelling and grammar could be better, but I'm just heading into ninth grade. I'll learn all the stupid rules eventually.

The knocking stops, and I blow out a relieved

breath. With any luck, Dan—God, I hate that name—will spend our allocated hour looking for me in all the nooks and crannies of our two-story Moscow penthouse before calling it quits for the day. He might complain to my father too, but whatever. I'd rather Papa yell at me than deal with Dan always looking at me *that way*.

I shudder as I recall that look. I see it on male faces all the time now that I've sprouted boobs. They're not big or anything—some of the girls in my class are already a D-cup or above—but boys don't seem to mind. Neither do grown men, especially when Mama makes me wear makeup. Speaking of which—

Another knock falls on my door, this one much more insistent. I recognize its cadence even through the music blaring in my earbuds. Reluctantly, I pause the game and turn down the volume on my iPod. "Yeah?"

"Alinochka, it's me. Are you all dressed and ready?"

Ugh, I was hoping she'd forget about me. Pulling out my earbuds, I shut off the TV and jump up. "One sec, Mama!"

Ignoring that, she pushes open the door and steps into my room. Instantly, her eyes widen. "What are you wearing?"

Busted. I glance down at my sweatpants and oversized T-shirt with as much nonchalance as I can muster. "Clothes."

She narrows her eyes. "Don't get smart with me. You know what I'm asking."

"Fine." I heave an exasperated sigh. "Just give me a minute."

"You have thirty seconds," she calls as I run into my closet and throw on the first dress I can find that she'll likely deem appropriate—a red evening gown that's as sparkly as it is uncomfortable.

I don't know why I have to wear this crap every time Papa has guests over, but Mama insists. Something about putting our best foot forward. Except in this dress, it's more like my best boob forward. Seriously, have they grown bigger since last week? Grimacing, I try to shove the swells of flesh deeper into the corset-like bodice, but the built-in pushup bra does its job too well.

"What are you doing? Stop that. It's supposed to look like that," Mama says, entering the closet to swat my hands away. "Now put on some shoes, and we'll do your hair and makeup."

Shoot me now. I put on a pair of high-heeled platforms that match the dress and let her shepherd me to the mirror, where she begins brushing my long hair with all the speed and enthusiasm of someone determined to rip it out by the roots.

"Ouch!" I wince as the brush catches on a particularly brutal knot, but she ignores me again. I guess that's what I get for leaving this until the last minute.

Finally, my hair is smooth and straight. I wish I could pull it into a ponytail, but Mama likes it hanging down my back in a jet-black curtain. I'm not a fan of the color and dream of the day when I'll be allowed to add some highlights. Next year, hopefully.

Makeup is next. Glumly, I watch as my pale face is brightened with a blush, my lips are transformed into a shiny red pout, and the catlike tilt of my green eyes is emphasized with a skillful application of liner and mascara. The only imperfection left is in my smile, with the little gap between my front teeth that Mama says makes me look "distinctive."

"There, much better," she says with satisfaction when she's done, and it's all I can do not to grimace.

The girl looking back at me in the mirror isn't a stranger so much as someone I don't like. All glossy and fake and *adult.* With my above-average height and my dress clinging to my newly sprouted curves, I look at least seventeen this way, maybe even eighteen. If Dan sees me like this, he'll choke on his drool. So will some of Papa's guests, those old men with their smarmy compliments whom he likes to parade me in front of.

I hate it. I hate being this shiny, pretty object that Mama and Papa trot out like a prized pony. If I had my way, I'd live in my sweatpants and T-shirts, playing *Mario* and *Zelda* and listening to Kanye all day long. But that's not the life of a Molotov. We're the cream of the crop, or at least the oil scum floating in a pot of soup. High society, as Mama likes to call it—or top of the mafia hierarchy, as I think of it.

Vladimir Molotov, my father, is filthy rich. The kind of rich that only gets to be that way in Russia through less-than-savory means. Mama thinks I don't know what kind of man he is—what kind of men he's raised my older brothers to be—but I do. I've been overhearing her fights with Papa my whole life. Fights that have gotten worse in recent years, though I try not to think about that.

"We should have you model," Mama says, stepping back to examine me approvingly, and this time, I do grimace.

I hope she's just saying it, but knowing my mom, she's already sent my pictures to some agency.

"Who's coming today?" I ask, just in case she hasn't yet sent the pictures. Maybe if I distract her, she'll forget this terrible idea altogether. "Papa's business partners?"

"Yes, and—"

"Vera!" Papa's deep voice booms from downstairs. "Where are you? They're here."

At the sound of her name, my mom smooths her palms over her dress and touches her elaborately coiled updo to make sure every single glossy brown hair is in place. "Coming!" she yells back before pinning me with a laser stare. "You will come down in a half hour to greet everyone, you hear? Keep an eye on the clock and don't go getting lost in those silly games of yours. This is important."

I roll my eyes. "Yeah, yeah."

"I mean it, Alina. I won't have time to come up here and drag you out."

"Yeah, I got it. Now go." I make shooing motions with my hands. "Papa is waiting."

With one last narrow-eyed look at me, she departs, and I plop onto the couch and turn on my game.

I'm so caught up in beating the next boss that by the time I look at the clock, it's been close to an hour. Oops. I run over to the mirror to make sure my makeup hasn't smeared, and then I hurry out of the room as fast as the stupid heels allow.

As I walk down the hallway, I catch a murmur of voices and drunken laughter coming from downstairs. I can picture the old men and their wives, all glammed up and perfumed, saying their cheesy toasts as they pound down vodka and cognac while devouring the rich spread of appetizers our chef, Pavel, has prepared. No basic *salat oliv'ye* here; it's all fancy caviar and gourmet French cheese, each dish carefully curated to show off our power and wealth.

I'm passing by Papa's study when the door swings open and a man steps out in front of me.

Startled, I jump back, and my left heel lands on the carpet the wrong way. I cry out, arms flailing as my ankle buckles painfully underneath me. Before I can fall on my ass, strong hands grab my elbows, stabilizing me, and I find myself looking up into the darkest pair of eyes I've ever seen.

The man holding me is muscular and tall. So tall

that even in my heels, I have to crane my neck to hold his gaze. And he's young. Young enough to be called a boy. His height and the breadth of his shoulders fooled me initially, but he can't be much older than my brother Nikolai, who's just turned twenty.

I swallow hard as those dark, hooded eyes rake over my face, lingering for a moment on my bright red lips. My heart is pounding and my skin feels strangely warm, especially where his fingers grip my bare arms. I've never been so physically close to a male who's unrelated to me, and while this man-boy is nowhere near as ridiculously handsome as my brothers, I can't stop staring at his face, with its rugged, potently masculine features. There's something wild about him, something untamed in the tousled black locks falling over his forehead and in the sharp, almost cruel lines of his jaw. Even his cologne, with its subtle notes of pine and leather, reminds me of dark winter forests and the dangers lurking within.

"You okay?" he asks softly. The deep timbre of his voice is that of a man, not a boy. "Did you hurt yourself?"

I manage a headshake, and he lets go of me. I immediately step back. My arms tingle where he held me, the cool air wafting over my skin forming a stark contrast to the heat of his touch.

He runs his gaze over me, the look in it distinctly male and adult. Strangely, I don't mind. For the first time, I'm glad I look all of seventeen, maybe even eighteen. I wish I looked twenty. Pulling back my shoulders, I stand straighter, even as a trickle of nervous sweat runs down my spine underneath the tight bodice of the dress.

Does he like what he sees? Because I want him to. I want it badly.

His lips curl wickedly as his eyes return to my face. "What's the matter, beauty? Cat got your tongue?"

Beauty? He does like what he sees! Then the meaning of his words filters into my brain, and I realize I've been staring at him in total silence, like an awestruck groupie. A hot flush scorches my face. "Of course not!"

His eyes narrow, the wicked smirk falling off his lips, and I want to crawl under the carpet. What a stupid, immature response. Worse yet, the words came out in a squeak, making me sound like a dumb kid instead of a young adult close to his age. Which is what I'll be soon-ish. Like in four or five years.

Clearing my throat, I pitch my voice deeper. "What the hell are you doing up here?"

There. That sounded like a maybe-eighteen-year-old. One with attitude. I think older boys like that.

A speculative gleam appears in his eyes, mixing with a hint of amusement. "What are *you* doing up here?"

I scoff. "Nice try. That's my room back there." I jab my thumb toward my bedroom and channel Papa at his bossiest. "Now answer my question. What are you doing in my father's office?"

His voice goes ice cold. "Your father's?" A hard

mask drops over his face, all hints of boyishness disappearing from his features. The man looking at me now is as dark and dangerous as any of my father's enforcers. "*You're* Alina? Molotov's thirteen-year-old daughter?"

"I'm almost fourteen!" Dammit, that came out sounding like I'm all of ten. So much for convincing him I'm close to his age, whatever that is. Calling upon generations of Molotov arrogance, I ask as haughtily as I can manage, "How old are *you*?"

In truth, I'm not sure I want to know anymore. Or to be anywhere near him. While the boy intrigued me, the man scares me. There's derision in his dark, almost-black eyes as he stares at me now. Derision and something else... something frightening.

His voice turns lethally soft. "That's none of your business, little girl. Run to your father and tell him his plan didn't work. I'm not taking the bait, no matter how prettily packaged it may be."

Bait? What is he—?

Then it dawns on me. He's referring to *me*.

I'm the prettily packaged bait.

My face turns hot again, but this time with pure, undiluted anger. "Fuck you. I'm no bait."

"Aren't you?" He rakes his gaze over me, a cruel curve appearing on his lips. "Why else would they dangle you in front of me dressed like that?"

"Nobody's dangling me!" I want to slap him. I want to claw his eyes out. Mama likes me to look pretty, true, but it's a status thing for her and Papa. Like the caviar and the fancy cheese. My brothers have to dress up when we have company too; that's just how we were raised. Fuming, I pointedly drag my gaze over him, from the top of his black hair to the shiny tips of his shoes. "Are they dangling *you?*"

Because he's dressed in evening attire also. I'm so used to seeing men in tuxes and suits that I didn't register his clothes at first. But they're nice, as fancy as anything my father and brothers wear. His black tuxedo jacket hugs his broad shoulders before tapering into his lean waist, and his pants fit his long, athletic legs perfectly. His shirt is a crisp, gleaming white, highlighting the olive hue of his skin and the stark black of his bowtie. And above it—wait, is that a tattoo peeking out of the starched collar of his shirt?

He gives a short, sharp bark of laughter, but there's no amusement in the sound, nothing but that cruel derision. "Clever child, aren't you? A Molotov in the truest sense of the word."

I grit my teeth. "I'm not a child." Then I process the second part of his remark, and a peculiar suspicion sprouts within me. I narrow my eyes. "Who are you again?"

He gives me a mocking bow. "Alexei Leonov, at your service."

And with that bombshell, he turns on his heel and heads toward the stairs as if he has every right to be here.

I'm still in shock as Papa introduces me to the guests sitting around the long dining table while Mama casts me looks that promise retribution for my lateness. None of my brothers are here today. Nikolai is serving in the army, Konstantin flat-out refuses to come to these events, and Valery is attending summer school in Amsterdam. Good for them. I wish I were anywhere but here, with *him*.

Alexei Leonov.

He's not here by himself either. His father, Boris, is also my parents' guest tonight, which is about as insane as the Montagues hosting the Capulets. Okay, maybe that's too dramatic—we're not actively at war with the Leonovs, and I'm certainly no Juliet—but our families are far from friendly. The animosity goes all the way back to the time when Alexei's grandfather framed mine for disloyalty to the Communist regime and got him sent away to a Siberian labor camp. My grandfather somehow made it out after two years and promptly turned the tables on his enemy, getting *him* sent away to the labor camp on a similarly trumped-up charge.

Yep, good old Soviet fun.

In any case, the Leonovs are bad news. That's been drilled into me since I was old enough to walk. They may be almost as rich and powerful as we are, but they lack our sophistication and polish. They're basically extremely wealthy thugs, their wealth acquired through even more unsavory means than ours. In the past, a fair amount of blood was spilled between our families' underlings, and in recent years, Papa would often come home in a terrible mood because of something the Leonovs had done, like undercutting him on a business deal or sabotaging some factory.

All of this is to say that I have no idea why the Leonovs are here and why Papa is introducing me to his sworn enemy as if they were best friends.

"—is my youngest," he's saying proudly to Boris when I tune back in. "Gorgeous, isn't she?"

"She's going to be a model," Mama chimes in. "All the agencies are interested in her."

Fuck. She did send in the pictures. Well, whatever. I have no intention of modeling anything. When I grow up, I'm going to be a video game developer. Konstantin is already teaching me some basic coding skills.

"Yes, beautiful," Boris agrees in a gravelly voice, dispassionately studying me with eyes as dark as his son's.

An involuntary shudder skates down my spine. If Alexei scared me a bit toward the end, this man downright terrifies me. I know now what I saw in Alexei's eyes besides derision. I know it because his father radiates it.

Cruelty. Darkness. I feel it as viscerally as the cold caress of a blade.

Now that I'm meeting the man, I believe every scary rumor about him—and about his sons. Especially Alexei, the older one.

I've been trying to avoid looking at him, but something keeps drawing my gaze to his face—a face as hard and impassive as his father's. There's no trace of recognition in his cold, dark eyes, no hint that we've already met and that he'd kept me from falling on my ass and called me "beauty."

Just thinking about it makes my arms tingle where he gripped me.

By all rights, I should tell Papa about seeing Alexei upstairs in his office, but for some reason, I can't bring myself to do so. Everything about that encounter has unsettled me, to the point that all I want is to survive these introductions and go hide out in my room.

Alas, that's not to be. As soon as the introductions are over, Mama makes me sit beside her at the table while Papa launches into a long toast about partnerships, friendships, and all kinds of bullshit. Worse yet, the entire time I have to fight the urge to stare at Alexei, who's acting like I don't exist. Ignoring me completely, he converses with a middle-aged man sitting to the right of him. Ivan somebody—a politician, I think. I zoned out during most of the introductions.

Mama plates some food for me and pours me a glass of wine, so I can toast alongside the adults. I dutifully take a sip when Papa finally finishes the toast, and then I pick at my food for the next half hour, my appetite nonexistent.

"Alinochka, why aren't you eating?" Mama asks with a frown when she notices.

I shrug. "You want me to be a model, don't you? Models don't eat."

She gives me a dark look, and I know that if it weren't for all the people sitting around us, she'd rip me a new one. As is, she smiles tightly, as if I've just made a joke, and changes the subject to our upcoming vacation in Cyprus.

I pick at my food some more, mostly for Pavel, who worked hard to prepare these dishes, and then I excuse myself to use the restroom. I'm hoping nobody notices when I don't return. By now, most of the people here are three sheets to the wind with all the nonstop toasts.

Most but not all. As I'm leaving, I catch Alexei's eyes on me—icy dark and not the least bit inebriated.

I guess he does know I exist.

My chest feels tight as I run up the stairs and hurry to my room. It's not until I shut the door behind me that I'm able to take a full breath. Plopping onto my couch, I put in my earbuds and turn on my game, but it doesn't help.

When I fall asleep two hours later, I'm still thinking about our encounter, still feeling unsettled and strangely unsafe.

Chapter 3

Present Day, Location Unknown

I wake up to blinding sunshine and the sound of ocean waves.

Wait, ocean waves? What the fuck?

I open my eyes, a move that proves surprisingly easy. My eyelids no longer feel welded together, nor does my body feel extra heavy, though my mouth is painfully dry. Whatever drug I was given has worn off.

Blinking against the bright light, I take in my surroundings.

I'm in a large, sunlit room with several circular windows. The walls are all gleaming blond wood, as is the ceiling. The furniture in the room, made of the same wood, is minimal: a dresser, a nightstand, a lounge chair in the corner, and the spacious bed I'm lying on, which is covered with white sheets. High-end Scandinavian, that's the vibe I'm getting—along with a touch of nausea generated by the gentle rocking underneath me.

A boat. I must be on a boat.

I sit up slowly, holding the top sheet against my chest. I'm dressed in something light and silky—a peignoir. Since the last thing I remember wearing is a red evening gown, someone must've changed my clothes, and I know exactly who that someone is. My heart rate picks up, my insides contracting into a knot even as my thoughts remain oddly calm and orderly.

My first step is to determine if I am indeed on a boat. I cast a look around and am relieved to find a peach-colored silk robe hanging on a hook on the back of a door to my left. It looks like something I might buy myself, as does the pale peach peignoir I'm wearing.

I'm not surprised. Alexei knows my tastes.

Swinging my feet to the floor, I swallow against the dryness in my throat, and my gaze falls on the bottle of water on the nightstand. I grab it and greedily gulp it down.

There. Much better.

I set down the empty bottle, slide my feet into a pair of elegant house slippers—again similar to the ones I favor—and walk over to the door to get the robe. I'm still strangely calm. Maybe the drug hasn't worn off entirely?

Grabbing the robe, I belt it around my waist and step over to one of the windows.

It's as I thought. Nothing but blue water in sight.

My heart gives an uneven thump, and tension gathers at my temples.

No. Not the headache. I can't deal with that right now.

I take a deep breath and force my facial muscles to soften. I'm calm. All calm and Zen. Sure, I'm somewhere in the middle of the ocean with the man who's terrified me for the past decade, but that doesn't mean I have to panic, does it? Panic won't accomplish anything. I need to think. I need to focus.

Only my body is not listening. My heart is full-on galloping, and my hands are beginning to tremble.

Alexei Leonov has me in his grasp, and nothing and no one can save me.

I drag another deep breath into my lungs and walk over to a different window, just in case I might be able to spot land from there.

Nope. Blue ocean all the way to the horizon. A somewhat unsettled ocean, too. I can see the white crests on the waves and feel the boat rocking underneath me. My nausea abruptly intensifies, and I turn away from the window before I get seasick.

I don't need that either. At all.

What I do need is a bathroom, and that need is growing more urgent by the second.

I hurry over to the door where the robe was hanging and turn the knob. Score. A bathroom. A nice, luxurious one, again with that upscale Scandinavian vibe. In addition to a large shower stall, there is a clawfoot tub by another circular window that lets in a ton of light.

After I take care of my most pressing needs, I locate

a brand-new electric toothbrush—the same kind I used in Moscow—and brush my teeth. Then I hop into the shower, even though I don't feel the least bit grimy. Which is strange, come to think of it. It's been anywhere from several hours to several days since Alexei took me from my brother's compound, so I should be at least somewhat unclean.

He must've washed me when he changed my clothes. That's the only explanation.

My breathing quickens, and it's all I can do to hang on to whatever shreds of calmness remain. I've been trying not to think about Alexei's hands on me, undressing me and fitting the peignoir onto my naked body, but I can't keep the images of him bathing me out of my mind.

The images and the disturbing way they make me feel.

With the thought of him in mind, I hurry through the shower, not bothering to wash my hair even though the corner shelf is stocked with my favorite brand of shampoo and conditioner. Instead, I quickly soap up my body and wash my face, and then I step out and dry myself with a fluffy towel that also looks suspiciously like the ones I had back home.

I don't want to put the worn peignoir back on, so I wrap another towel around my torso and smooth my slightly damp hair with a boar-bristle brush—identical to the one I like, of course. A search of the vanity drawers reveals my favorite brands of skincare, makeup, and hair-styling tools. After a moment of hesitation, I avail myself of everything because I feel better, more in control, when I have my beauty mask on.

When I'm done, I look exactly like I always do: flawless skin, red lipstick, cat-eye liner. My vampire-black hair is long and straight, flat-ironed to a smooth gloss. All I need now are my designer clothes, and I'll feel completely like myself. Or at least the self I've carefully cultivated over the past few years.

Clutching the towel tightly around my chest, I exit into the bedroom—and freeze in place.

Like a demon summoned by my earlier thoughts about him, Alexei Leonov stands in front of me, a cruel smile dancing on his lips.

Chapter 4

10 Years and 9 Months Earlier, Moscow

"I hate winter holidays," I tell Konstantin as he sets up my new gaming computer. "I really do."

His gaze doesn't leave the screen as his fingers fly over the keyboard. "You hate seeing me?"

"No, silly, not you." My oldest brother is my favorite, in fact. "I'm talking about *that*." I circle my finger in the air to indicate the raised voices filtering into my room through the air vent.

My parents think that because the walls in our penthouse are thick, nobody can hear them fighting, but I can. I always hear them.

Konstantin finally looks at me, his hazel eyes distracted behind his glasses. "Ah, yes, that."

He goes back to installing the software, and I plop onto my bed with a sigh. As much as I love Kostya, his emotional IQ is far below his genius-level general intelligence. I sometimes wonder if he's on the spectrum, like that kid in my class who's brilliant but socially challenged. Then again, this could just be how my brother deals with the pressure of being the oldest Molotov son—by opting out of the whole thing altogether. Luckily for my parents, they have Nikolai, who thrives on all the wheeling, dealing, and other business bullshit, and Valery, who, while strange in his own way, displays the Machiavellian traits that Papa adores.

Me, I'm just the daughter. All that's expected of me is to look pretty and eventually marry well, so the Molotovs become even richer and better connected. Yay for feminism. Maybe in another century or so, it'll reach our social circle in Moscow. Of course, I'm a shitty daughter, so I don't plan to do what's expected of me. I've already refused the stupid agency's offer to model for them—something Mama had a fit over, but whatever—and I'm certainly not marrying some annoying politician just so that Papa can secure another government contract.

I'm going to attend college in the States, study computer science, and get a job at a video game company like Nintendo. Preferably in Japan or some other cool place. Russia is so not my jam.

An alarm goes off on my phone, startling me.

Oh, crap. I almost forgot. *Dan.*

"What's that?" Konstantin asks absentmindedly, and I sigh, silencing the alarm.

"My English lesson, what else?"

One measly C on an essay, and this is the result: an hour-long session with Dan every day over the holidays. I get straight A's in math and science, but not in English—probably because I prefer to read in Russian. I find English grammar and spelling patterns as incomprehensible as the workings of Valery's mind.

Grudgingly, I pull on my sweatshirt and head to the library downstairs, where Dan is waiting for me. Mama told me that if I skip these lessons, I won't be returning to my boarding school in New Hampshire this upcoming semester. She'll enroll me in a school in Moscow instead, since, and I quote, "You're clearly wasting your time in America." Never mind that my American peers can't even tell that I'm from Russia when they speak to me, or that plenty of them get C's or worse on their essays and exams. Oh, no, my written English must be perfect, or else I'm "wasting" time.

Yeah, whatever.

Dan jumps up as soon as I enter the library, a wide grin on his freckled face. "There you are. I was worried you weren't feeling well again."

"Nope, the headache is gone," I say, fighting the urge to roll my eyes as he pulls out a chair for me, all gentleman-like. Since that chair is right next to him, I pointedly pull out a different one for myself across the table. This way, he can gawk at me, but not do those accidental elbow and hand brushes that creep me out so much.

Seriously, why are men such creeps?

I suppose, objectively speaking, Dan Sutter isn't ugly. He's somewhere in his mid-twenties and looks like the grown version of Ron from *Harry Potter*. He works as an aide at the US embassy and tutors rich Russian kids on the side. Mama met him at one of those political functions she and Papa often attend.

I've contemplated telling her about Dan's crush on me, or at least mentioning it to Konstantin, but I don't want word to get back to Papa and Nikolai. I can't forget what happened when I was twelve, after one of our bodyguards walked in on me changing and stayed a few seconds too long.

The man didn't leave the hospital for several months afterward.

I don't want that to happen to Dan. Not even if he's a bit of a creep. Instead, I do whatever I can to avoid these lessons, like faking headaches and pretending to forget about the time—a strategy that, unfortunately, Mama has caught on to. Hence the threat to take me out of my boarding school and make me live here full-time.

Yeah, no, thanks. I'd rather put up with an hour of Dan every day over the holidays than listen to Mama and Papa fighting year-round.

"Today, we'll tackle dangling modifiers," Dan says, and I suppress a groan.

Why? Why does anyone give a shit about this? Who cares if the modifier dangles—whatever that means?

Nevertheless, I dutifully follow along as Dan goes over what constitutes a "modifier" and why it's a bad thing when it "dangles." I think I'm starting to get it. Maybe. It's such a boring topic that even though Dan talks with the enthusiasm of an auctioneer hyping up a priceless painting, I have to fight the urge to yawn. To help myself concentrate, I stare at Dan's freckled hands as he waves them about, specifically at the big, gaudy ring on his right middle finger. It's one of those class or club rings. Dan's is from a Yale fraternity, and he must be really proud that he's an alum because he wears the stupid thing all the time.

The sounds of voices in the hallway reach my ears, distracting me for a moment. Does Papa have guests again?

"Here," Dan says, bringing my attention back to him. "See if you can find the dangling modifiers and fix them." He slides a sheet of paper across the table toward me.

I sigh and begin reading the sentences printed on it. *Being a princess, her hands were pretty and white.* That looks fine to me. Unless... does that imply that it's her hands that are a princess? Yeah, maybe that's a dangling modifier. I circle the offending part of the sentence and write in the blank space below: *Being a princess, she has hands that are pretty and white.*

Yep. That sounds better. Nailed it.

I go through a few more examples, and when I look up, Dan is staring at me with drool running down his chin. Okay, not literally, but that's basically what his expression is saying. Which is just ridiculous because I'm not wearing any makeup, my hair is in a messy bun, and my clothes are completely shapeless. Mama would have a fit if she saw me like this, but I'm doing Dan a favor.

I really don't want him to end up in a hospital or worse.

"What?" I snap when he continues staring, and he blinks like a startled frog.

"Oh, nothing. Just—you have something on your cheek."

I do? I rub my left cheek. "Better now?"

"No, it's the other—here." Before I can react, he reaches across the table and touches my other cheek. "Just this tiny bit of lint that's—"

With a faint squeak of hinges, the library door behind me swings open, and Dan jerks back as if stung by a jellyfish. Thank God. I'm not a violent person, but I was about to slap his hand away.

I turn around in my chair, expecting to see Mama checking up on us, but instead, I meet a pair of near-black eyes that have been on my mind more times since last summer than I'd care to admit.

"Excuse me," Alexei Leonov says evenly. "I didn't realize this room was occupied."

Unlike the last time I saw him, he's dressed casually, in a pair of dark jeans and a black T-shirt, the crewneck collar of which reveals a portion of a tattoo snaking up the side of his neck. A T-shirt, in the dead of winter. Did he take off his sweater along with his coat, or does he think he's immune to the freezing cold outside? My gaze falls on his tan, muscular arms, decorated with intricate tattoos as well, and my breath quickens, my heart taking on a heavy, thumping rhythm. Belatedly, I register that underneath one of those arms, he's holding a laptop—likely his reason for seeking out this room with its comfortable table and chairs.

Except… why would he work on his laptop in *our* library? Or be in *our* penthouse, for that matter?

How deep does Papa's newfound friendship with the Leonovs go?

Returning my gaze to Alexei's face, I lift my chin and say as coolly as I can manage, "It *is* occupied, as you can see."

I expect him to be looking at me, but he's not. It's Dan who commands his attention.

Dan, who's turned so red that his freckles are barely visible.

"W-we're in the middle of an English lesson," he stutters out in awkwardly accented Russian. "So if you d-don't mind…"

Alexei doesn't move. His hard features are expressionless, but whatever Dan sees in his eyes makes my tutor's face shift from the color of boiled lobster to that of a drowned cadaver.

Normally, I'd revel in Dan's discomfort, but right now, the hair on my nape rises. Because I feel it. *Menace.* It rolls off Alexei in waves. That sense of danger, of barely leashed violence, is so palpable I already smell blood in the air.

I have no idea what's happening or why, but I know I have to put a stop to it. Now. Before that violence is unleashed. My heart thuds audibly against my ribcage as I say, "You can leave now."

My tone is imperious, but my voice comes out a pitch too high. Alexei wouldn't dare hurt me—probably—but I can't vouch for what he might do to my tutor.

Did he see Dan touch me? Is that what this is all about?

Those dark eyes swing my way, and cold sweat gathers under my armpits. Only six months have passed since I saw him last, but there's nothing of the boy left in Alexei Leonov. His jaw is even harder, more cruelly defined, his cheeks leaner and his cheekbones more prominent. There's no trace of softness in his icy gaze, no hint of the flirtatiousness that marked the beginning of our first encounter. The man in front of me is cold and lethal, as dangerous as the Leonovs are known to be. I feel it deep in my bones.

Calling upon all of my courage, I say again, "Leave. Right now. We're busy."

Something dark flits over Alexei's face, but he inclines his head. "As you wish."

He exits, closing the door behind him, and for the first time since he walked in, I'm able to draw in a full breath.

I'm not the only one, either. When I turn back to face Dan, he's regaining some of his color. He's even attempting a smile, as if he didn't almost shit his pants a minute ago. And suddenly, I've had enough.

Before I can think through all the potential consequences, I paste on a sweet smile and lean forward. "You'd better pray he doesn't talk to my father or brothers. I don't know how much you've heard about my family, but they are *not* like your other employers."

Dan's face goes white, red, and back to white, all in the span of five seconds. "I-I don't know what you're talking about."

My smile widens. "Don't you?"

Fuck, this is fun. Why haven't I done this sooner? Why did I decide that my only options were to tell my family and risk Dan's life, or to tolerate his lecherous looks and gross little touches? There was always a third option, and now that I've realized that, I feel a ton lighter. I suppose I should thank Alexei for showing me the power of fear.

If I hadn't seen Dan stuttering and scared shitless at the mere thought that he might've been seen touching me, it would've taken me way longer to realize that I can threaten him into doing—or not doing—whatever I want.

Sure enough, my tutor swallows, his Adam's apple bobbing. "I-I'm sorry. It won't happen again."

No, it won't. I've made sure of that.

The next day, I find myself almost looking forward to my English lesson. After our little chat, Dan had kept his hands and eyes to himself, to the point that I had to call his name to get him to look my way—and even then, he was all pale and prone to stuttering.

I like it. I like it a lot. This must be what it feels like

to have power, to know that you're the one in control. It's a new experience for me. All my life, I've been told what to do, what to wear, where to go to school, and how to act. My parents, my teachers, my brothers—they all have power and authority over me. So did Dan, up until yesterday. Maybe that's why it didn't occur to me that I could do something to change our dynamic on my own, without relying on my father or brothers.

I all but dance to the library when it's time for the lesson. On the agenda today is the Oxford comma—and testing the limits of my newfound power over Dan. To that end, I've omitted my usual baggy sweatshirt and sweatpants in favor of a pair of skinny jeans and a tight V-neck shirt. It's not exactly a fancy designer dress of the kind Mama likes me to wear, but I look good. I'm even wearing a light layer of makeup, which she'd approve of.

I want Dan to be tempted to stare but be too afraid to do it. It's my little revenge on him for all those times when I felt like I needed to shower after our lessons.

I must be early for once because Dan isn't in the library when I enter. I wait a few minutes, glancing at the clock every so often, but he doesn't appear.

Huh. Maybe I scared him off for good?

I give it another ten minutes, and then I go in search of my mom.

I find her in the kitchen, fighting with Papa over something. Hearing their voices, I stop before entering and listen, in case I'm walking in on something major. But no. They're arguing about tonight's menu, it seems.

That's not too bad. Or maybe it is. They fight over everything these days. Each time I come home after being away at school, I find them even more at each other's throats. The sad part is I'm pretty sure they love each other, or at least Papa loves Mama. I often see him looking at her like he'd like to chain her to his side. Then again, maybe that's not love. At least not the kind they write about in books and portray in movies. It's more like he can't live without her, and there's a part of him that hates that fact—and her. As for Mama, I can't decide if she actually hates him, or if it's all part of some cruel game they're playing. Sometimes, I catch *her* looking at him like he's her entire world, but other times, I'm almost certain she wishes him dead.

Yeah, my family is lovely. All nice and normal and sweet.

The argument in the kitchen seems to be dying down, so I decide to risk it. Rounding the corner behind which I've been hiding, I call out, "Mama? Did Dan say anything about cancelling our lesson today?" Stopping by the kitchen island, I blink exaggeratedly. "Oh, hi, Papa. Didn't know you were there."

Someone give me an Oscar.

Pavel, our chef who's also our housekeeper, occasional bodyguard, and even more occasional enforcer, shoots me a sidelong glance from the counter where he's chopping up vegetables for dinner. He's not fooled. He probably heard me coming before I even exited the library.

I give him a bright smile. Pavel is my favorite

person here—at least if I exclude Konstantin. Actually, my oldest brother no longer resides with us, so I don't need to qualify that statement. Pavel is former military —he served with Papa long before I was born, in fact— and he still has all the habits and mannerisms he picked up in the army. He runs our household like a drill sergeant, with set mealtimes and so on. He's also the size of a small truck, has a face that resembles a battered brick, and seems to possess all the emotions of a machine. But that last bit is a façade. I'll never forget all the times he bandaged my scraped knees when I was a kid, nor all the treats he snuck up to my room when I was upset over something.

I think of him as my giant, not-so-cuddly teddy bear… who can kill on command.

"Alinochka, you look so nice," Mama exclaims, giving my outfit an approving once-over. "Is that shirt new?"

Papa glares at her. "All her clothes are new, just like yours. None of you wear perfectly good shit twice."

Well, he's in a mood. I can hear the unspoken "ungrateful bitches" after that "you." I used to wonder why Mama doesn't just leave him, but now that I'm older, I understand that she can't. Even if they didn't have this messed-up love-hate connection, it's not up to her.

He wouldn't let her go.

"Don't you dare use that kind of language around our daughter," Mama hisses at him. "If she wants new clothes every day, she can fucking have them!"

Ugh. Here we go again. My shirt actually isn't new—I've worn it a bunch of times at school—but anything I say in that regard will only add fuel to this shitstorm.

Papa opens his mouth, undoubtedly to light into her over *her* language, so I say quickly, "Mama, I was asking about Dan. He hasn't shown up for our lesson."

She goes from glaring at Papa to frowning at me. "He hasn't?"

"No. Did he say he couldn't make it today?" I'm tempted to ask if he quit, but that could result in all sorts of uncomfortable questions.

"He didn't, no," Mama says, her frown deepening. She turns to Papa. "You didn't hear anything, right?"

"No," he says, his upper lip curling. "Why would I?"

"Oh, I don't know. Maybe because it's your daughter's education on the line—not that you give a fuck, you selfish bastard."

And that's my cue to leave. Making a face at Pavel, who's looking at me sympathetically, I slip out of the kitchen and head upstairs to my room. I can't wait for this stupid winter vacation to end. Being with my parents is the worst. Sometimes, I wonder how they even got together in the first place. Sure, Papa is ridiculously handsome in the way that all Molotov men are—even at his age, women stare at him like he's their favorite flavor of ice cream—but Mama is beautiful too, and I'm sure she had options.

I used to think it was somehow my fault, their constant fights, but in recent years, I've come to the conclusion that they're just toxic together. That their love, if that's what it is, is poison at its core.

Sometimes I wonder if that poison has infected me... if I'm destined for an equally toxic relationship.

It's not until an hour later, when I'm finishing up another level of *Zelda,* that my thoughts return to Dan. Why didn't he show up? Even if I scared him off, shouldn't he have called with some kind of an excuse? You don't just flake on the Molotovs on a whim, at least not if you have any brains.

I go looking for my mom again, and this time, I get lucky and find her in the media room, watching a soap opera by herself.

"Any news on Dan?" I ask.

She pauses the TV and shakes her head. "I've tried calling him, but he's not picking up. It goes straight to voicemail. I reached out to our contacts at the US embassy, but they said they haven't heard from him either. He didn't come to work today."

Huh. Against my will, my mind flashes back to the menace emanating from Alexei yesterday, and a chill roughens the skin on my arms. Could Alexei have said something to my father yesterday? Or, even less likely, could he have done something to Dan himself? I don't see why he'd do either—I'm nobody to him—but maybe evil doesn't need a reason.

Maybe Dan is at the bottom of the Moscow River as we speak.

"Thanks, Mama," I say as steadily as I can. "Let me know if you hear anything."

"Of course." She resumes her show. "Your father is already looking into it."

That's good. We should hear something soon, then.

I return to my room and play my game some more before getting on a chat with my friends from boarding school. That occupies me until it's time to go to sleep. It's a restless sleep, filled with unsettling dreams about black, demonic eyes, and the next morning, I wake up tired and lethargic.

"Anything?" I ask Mom over breakfast, and she shakes her head, looking puzzled.

"It's like he's disappeared into thin air."

My stomach tightens, and the peanut butter toast I've just bitten into tastes like sawdust. I know the kind of resources Papa has, and if he still hasn't learned anything about Dan's disappearance, there can be only two reasons for that.

He's either not looking, because he's the one who made him disappear, or he's up against someone with comparable resources.

Like the Leonovs.

"I'm going to walk to Natasha's," I say, pushing my plate away. "I've got a headache, and fresh air might help."

It's not a lie this time. I feel a band of pressure around my temples, a band that tightens more with each passing second. It's an unfamiliar sensation, and one that I definitively dislike.

"Of course," Mama says. "Pavel is busy, but a couple of guards will go with you."

I nod and hurry to get dressed. I need to get out of here before my head explodes. I text Natasha as I'm pulling on my coat. She replies right away, as expected. My friend is always down to hang, but even if she weren't, I'd use the excuse of visiting her to get out of the house.

It's freezing outside when I exit our high-rise building, the guards following me at a discreet distance, as always. The cold air bites at the exposed parts of my face, but I don't mind. It's cold in New Hampshire in the winter as well, so I'm used to it.

Natasha's building is only a few blocks away, yet I'm feeling better by the end of the walk. As I hoped, breathing in the fresh, crisp air has chased away the worst of the pressure around my skull. Maybe I'm worrying over nothing. Dan could've just had some family emergency and hopped on a plane back to the States without telling anyone, his work and tutoring employers included.

Yeah, right. And aliens landed in the Red Square yesterday. Not to mention, my father has undoubtedly checked all the flight records by now and would know if Dan simply went home.

If my father is looking, that is.

Pushing that unpleasant thought out of my mind, I enter Natasha's building and spend the next couple of hours hanging out at her apartment, gossiping about everyone we know. Her place is almost as nice as our penthouse, even though her parents aren't nearly as rich. They're multi-millionaires, but that's nothing in our circle. Some of the other girls look down on Natasha for that, but I've always liked her, ever since we attended the same exclusive kindergarten here in Moscow.

"You okay? You seem out of it," she says, and I realize I haven't answered her question about my spring break plans. She wants me to go to Ibiza with her, I think. Or is it Belize?

"Yeah, sorry. Just got poor sleep." I push my fingers through my hair. "I think I'm down. Mama told me last year I could go once I'm in high school, but I'll run it past her and let you know."

Natasha chews on a strand of her blond hair. "I really hope you can go. Kristina will be there. And Vitalik."

Of course. Vitalik, Natasha's crush since the third grade—who's currently dating Kristina, the bitchiest girl we know. Without me as a buffer, Kristina will eat Natasha alive.

"I'll do my best," I say and stand up from the couch, preparing to head out.

"Excuse me," a curvy blond woman says, entering the living room. She's the housekeeper—Lyudmila, I think. "There's a delivery for Alina Molotova."

"For me?" I blink at her. "But I don't live here."

She shrugs and hands me a black velvet box, the

kind that often contains jewelry. "The note said to give it to you, so here you go."

"Open it," Natasha urges. Her blue eyes sparkle with excitement. "Maybe it's from a secret admirer."

"Here in Moscow? Yeah, right." I wait for Lyudmila to leave, and then I carefully open the box.

Inside is a ring.

A big, gaudy male ring with the crest of a Yale fraternity.

The box drops from my nerveless fingers. The ring falls out of it and rolls across the floor.

"What is it?" Natasha asks, alarmed, but I'm already running out of the room, chasing Lyudmila.

"The note," I say urgently, catching up with her in the kitchen. "Where's the note?

"Oh, umm, hold on." She grabs it from a stack of papers on one of the counters. "Here you go."

I grab it and frantically scan it.

It's only two lines:

For Alina Molotova.

-AL

Chapter 5

Present Day, Location Unknown

"What are you doing here?" I ask, raising my chin.

I hate that my voice is shaking and my hands are frantically clutching at the edges of my towel as if I were a virginal maiden.

Which I actually am. He's ensured that.

The cruel curve of Alexei's lips deepens, dark amusement dancing in the depths of his eyes. "It's my boat."

"I meant here in my cabin." There, steadier now. Maybe I can still salvage this situation, buy myself a little more time.

He arches his eyebrows. "It's my cabin also."

My insides twist with fear and something far more unsettling. Simultaneously, my breathing picks up, my skin prickling with that dangerous heat I only ever feel around him. I'm acutely cognizant of his size and strength, of the way his thick muscles flex underneath the soft cotton of his black T-shirt and how his dark, well-worn jeans hug his powerfully built legs. Of the tattoos that cover his forearms, simultaneously concealing and emphasizing their sinewy strength.

He was intimidating at nineteen. Now, at thirty, he's a force to be reckoned with.

"Where are we?" I ask as evenly as I can. I don't want to delve deeper into the "my cabin" bit, don't want to think about what he means by that. I have a feeling I'll find out soon enough, but in the meantime, I need to get my bearings.

"We're on a boat," he answers, his eyes gleaming sardonically. "My boat."

I clench my jaw. "And where is the fucking boat?"

He tsk-tsks. "Such language."

"Fuck you."

"Oh, absolutely." He grins, flashing sharp teeth that appear extra white against the deep tan of his olive-hued skin. The Leonovs have some Sicilian blood in them, and it shows. His eyes rake over me, lingering on the spot where my hands are clutching the towel in a death grip. "Very soon."

My body goes simultaneously hot and cold, and I take an involuntary step back.

It's a mistake. Like a predator reacting to fleeing prey, he comes after me, advancing with lethally soft strides until he's right in front of me, so close I can smell his richly masculine cologne, with its signature notes of pine and leather. And ocean surf. The fresh, salty tang emanating from his skin is new, and it reminds me of where we are and how inescapable my new prison is.

Swallowing hard, I stare up into his hard-featured face as he lifts his hand and brushes my hair back, tucking it behind my ear. His touch burns like fire, adding to the turmoil inside me.

"My sweet beauty," he says softly. "Still think you can delay this, do you?"

I dampen my dry lips. I'm shaking deep inside, and I don't know if it's from trepidation or from the infernal heat consuming me. "I need more time. Please."

His eyes are almost pure black. "I've given you a decade."

Yes, he has. But it's not enough. A hundred years wouldn't be enough, and he knows it. What he wants is everything I fear and dread.

"Please," I try again, and whether it's the word itself or the tremor in my voice, his answering headshake is almost regretful. Almost sympathetic—even as his words slay me with all the mercilessness with which he murdered my brother's guards.

"No more waiting, Alinyonok." Covering my clenched hands with his big palms, he gently pries my fingers open, one by one, until the towel covering my body is held up only by the corner I tucked into the material over my breasts. I can feel it slowly slipping out, unraveling on its own, but he doesn't wait. Capturing both of my hands in one of his, he tugs on the towel, helping it along until it drops on the floor, leaving me standing naked in front of him.

The cool air flows over my freshly washed skin, adding to the sensation of icy-hot needles piercing my flesh and, perversely, the liquid heat gathering between my thighs. My nipples contract into stiff, aching points, and I have to fight not to sway helplessly toward him as he bends his head and imprints the words onto my ear with his warm breath. “It’s time you held up your end of our bargain.”

Chapter 6

10 Years and 1 Month Earlier, Moscow

Two weeks at home. That's all I have to tolerate this summer, thank fuck. Now that I've turned fifteen, Mama lets me travel with my friends—and our bodyguards, of course—and I spent all of June, July, and half of August exploring Italy, Greece, Spain, and France. I would've gladly continued on to Iceland with Natasha, but for some reason, my parents insisted that I return to Moscow—probably so I could witness more of their epic fights.

I try not to dwell on that, on the animosity between them that seems to grow every day, but it's impossible to ignore. I've been home less than a week, and I've already caught Mama crying twice. Papa isn't much better. He's drinking. And not the kind of drinking he's always done, where it's a glass or two of cognac after dinner or a few shots of vodka at a party. No, every day this summer, Papa has been drunk from noon onward—and I can't help but wonder if it's my fault.

Yesterday, through the vents in my bedroom, I heard Mama screaming at him, and I caught my name being mentioned. Why, I don't know, but I suspect it has something to do with what happened to Dan over the winter holidays. I didn't tell anyone in my family about receiving Dan's ring, but somehow, my father and my brothers found out. Most likely, Lyudmila, Natasha's housekeeper, said something to my guards. Or to Pavel.

Apparently, he's been seeing her for the past year. Mama told me so yesterday.

I don't want to think about Pavel with Lyudmila, or about anything to do with that winter break. It's been less than a month since I've stopped waking up in a cold sweat from a nightmare where Dan's corpse emerges from the Moscow River and waddles toward me, hands waving—minus the finger with the ring. Not that I have any reason to think he's in the river. His body hasn't been found, though I don't know if anyone has really looked.

After my father confronted me about the ring and the note, I had no choice but to tell him the full story, including the part about Dan's advances. Papa was beyond furious. A vase might've gone flying at one point. Unfortunately, most of his fury was directed not at me, but at my mom, for hiring Dan and making me take lessons with him. No matter how much I protested that *I* was the one at fault for not speaking up, Papa wouldn't listen.

Their fight that day was so awful I've blocked it out of my mind. Unfortunately, I can't block out the soul-crushing knowledge that a man I knew is dead because of me.

Alexei Leonov killed him.

I still don't understand his motivation. Not for that note, not for any of it. Nor do I understand Papa's reaction to Alexei's involvement. All three of my brothers were enraged to learn that Alexei took this upon himself instead of letting our family handle it, but Papa was strangely calm about it. "I'll talk to him," was all he said, and that was the last I heard of it.

I wish I could be that chill, but I'm not. Knowing that it was Alexei who made my tutor disappear torments me nearly as much as my guilt over Dan's death. Yes, Dan was a creep, but he didn't deserve whatever befell him at Alexei's hands. And it *was* Alexei's hands—that note made it crystal clear.

Why did he send it along with the ring? Even if he thought Dan deserved to be killed for touching me, why did he do it himself instead of simply saying something to my family?

The one and only explanation that comes to mind is so insane that I shut it down as soon as it invades my thoughts. I refuse to even entertain that possibility. It's true that in our world, men do these sorts of things when other men poach on their territory, be it business or women. But that's ridiculous.

There's no way Alexei thinks of me as his territory.

Still, my subconscious must've latched on to the idea because my other nightmares—the ones from which I wake up feeling strangely hot and uncomfortable—involve a black-eyed demon coming to claim me, his blood-stained hands embracing me and his wicked mouth smirking as he drags me down into his terrifying underworld.

I have only three days of my summer vacation left when Mama comes into my room. Her pretty face is unusually pale, her eyes red and swollen underneath her makeup. She must've had another major row with Papa.

"Alinochka, there's something your father and I need to speak to you about," she says, her voice scratchier than usual. "Get dressed and meet us in the library in a half hour, okay?"

I sit up straighter on the couch, my heart lurching into a faster beat. "Why? What's going on?"

She attempts a smile. "Nothing. We'll talk to you when you come down, okay? And do wear one of your nicer dresses, please. We have company."

She leaves, closing the door behind her, and I stare at it blankly before springing to my feet. I have no idea what's going on, but my stomach feels tight, my chest cold. This isn't usual. My parents don't do joint talks with me. If there's something they want, Mama always talks to me on her own. It must be something big. But what? If she hadn't mentioned company, I would've thought my parents were finally getting a divorce, but they wouldn't want witnesses to that talk. Unless it's lawyers? But why would they want me to look nice for that?

Moving on autopilot, I put on a dress. It's not one of my fancy evening gowns—it's only eleven in the morning—but it's cute, something I might wear to a pool party with my friends. I also apply a little makeup, just so I don't look so pale and scared. I used to hate makeup, but I'm beginning to understand its utility, to appreciate its ability to conceal signs of stress and sleepless nights.

There. I look decent. Now if only my hands weren't so icy. Thankfully, I still have a few minutes before I need to be downstairs, so I go into my bathroom and warm them under a stream of hot water.

Finally, it's time to head to the library. I put on a pair of platform heels that go with the dress and walk down the stairs. My heart is drumming in my ears, and my mind is spinning with all sorts of unpleasant possibilities.

What if they're pulling me out of my boarding school to make me attend a local one?

Or—oh, God—what if something's happened to someone in our family?

No. No way. Mama would just tell me. She wouldn't make a big production out of it. When my grandmother—Dad's mom—passed away from a heart attack five years ago, Mama told me right away. No, this is something else, something to do specifically with me.

I'm sick with nerves by the time I approach the library and knock on the door.

"Come in," Papa calls.

I enter. Immediately, my eyes fall on the two guests, and my pulse leaps into the stratosphere.

Alexei Leonov and his father.

They're sitting across the table from my parents, regarding me with nearly identical pairs of dark, cold eyes.

"Alinochka, please join us," Mama says, a bit unsteadily. "We have some good news to discuss."

I force my limbs to move. They feel odd, like they don't belong to me. It's as if I were wearing a suit of flesh and bones instead of inhabiting my body.

The suit obeys my instructions, though, and I sit next to Mama, my eyes glued to Alexei, who's sitting directly across from me. He stares back at me with an unreadable expression, his big hands interlaced on the table in front of him.

I swallow hard, fighting the urge to look away like a coward. Once again, his presence makes me feel alternately hot and cold. Has his face always been so hard and chiseled, or has he matured even more in the six months since I saw him last? I've been stalking him online, so I know he's just turned twenty. By a bizarre coincidence, we share a birthday—July 24th—which makes him exactly five years older than I am. If my grandmother were alive, she'd say this means that our fates are intertwined, the threads of our lives woven together since birth, but that's silly. I don't believe in any of those village superstitions.

Papa clears his throat, and I redirect my attention to him, grateful for an excuse to look away from Alexei's darkly magnetic stare.

"Alina," Papa says gravely. "You've met Boris Sergeyevich Leonov and his son, Alexei."

Years of politeness training propel my response. "Yes, of course. Hello again. It's nice to see you both."

The elder Leonov inclines his head with a thin-lipped smile that makes my skin crawl, but Alexei's expression doesn't shift in any way. Nor does he say anything back. He just watches me with that indecipherable look in his onyx eyes.

"As you know, our families have a history that goes way back," Papa says. "And a relationship that, at times, has been… contentious." What he really means is it's a miracle we're all sitting here together without bloodshed.

Some kind of response seems warranted, so I nod, pressing my hands together under the table. I still have no clue what this is all about, but my fingers feel icy again.

"Today's world is very different from that of our fathers," Papa continues. "It's both smaller and bigger. It presents new challenges and new opportunities. It would be foolish to let feuds of decades past stand in the way of all of us seizing those opportunities, don't you think?"

Is he asking *me*? I dart a glance at Mama, but she's looking straight ahead, her lips tight. Not knowing what else to do, I nod cautiously again.

"Good," Papa says. "You understand then. Our families need a fresh start, a way to mend old rifts and build strong foundations for the future. A future where, instead of being rivals, the Leonovs and the Molotovs are partners, standing together against this rapidly changing world."

I sneak another look at Mama. I don't understand why I'm here, why it sounds as if Papa is giving this speech to *me*. Shouldn't Nikolai be here instead, since he's the one Papa is grooming to take over the business? Or Konstantin as the oldest? Or even Valery, who may only be seventeen but is already scary good at all sorts of unsavory things?

Mama is still not looking at me, so I return my attention to Papa, who's droning on about the advantages of a Leonov-Molotov partnership, both from a financial and a political perspective. It boils down to all of us becoming even more rich and influential, as if the billions we currently have are not enough.

"So," Papa says in conclusion, "Boris Sergeyevich and I have talked it over, and we've come up with a solution that benefits everyone. The best way to move past old rifts is to build a bridge over them, one that would unite us for decades to come."

He looks at Alexei and his father, which forces me to do the same. Alexei's face remains unreadable, while Boris is still smiling in that unsettling way.

A bizarre suspicion stirs in my mind, making my stomach tighten. But no. There's no way. Not even our families are backward enough to—

"Children are our future," Papa says, and it's as if a yawning fissure opens underneath me, the earth parting with a roar that nearly drowns out the next words he says. Nearly, but not entirely. They still reach my ears, each one as impossible to process as the next. "You, your brothers, Alexei, and his siblings—you'll all be here long after Boris and I are gone. And your children will be here after you. That's why it's important that you and Alexei marry, that the bond our families form isn't just one of business contracts, but of blood."

"Marry?" My question emerges through numb lips as I meet Alexei's impassive stare. He doesn't look shocked by this. He knew this was coming. I tear my gaze away from him and turn to Papa, my voice rising in pitch. "What do you mean, 'marry?' I'm fifteen!"

"Not now, obviously," Boris says, his gravelly voice scraping over my nerve endings. "You're both too young. It'll be in a few years. In the meantime, you'll get to know each other."

"No. No way." My gaze flits between Boris and my parents as I look for a sign that they're joking, that this is a horrible prank they've decided to play on me for some unfathomable reason. Boris and Papa meet my eyes without blinking, while Mama keeps her gaze trained on the table. I grab her hand, forcing her to finally look at me. "Mama? Tell me this is not—"

"Alina." Papa's tone hardens. "This isn't up for debate."

"But—"

"It's for your own good, Alinochka." Mama's voice shakes, belying her words. Her eyes swim with tears as she looks at me. "It really is."

The roar in my ears intensifies. They mean it. This isn't a joke. They intend to marry me off to Alexei. My eyes land on his face, which is still wearing that fucking unreadable mask, and it's all I can do not to reach across the table and shake him, to tell him to speak up and say that this is insane, that there's no way this is happening. But he doesn't say anything. Which means it's up to me. I jump to my feet. "No! No fucking way. I'm not doing it."

Papa stands up, his expression darkening. "This is not up for debate, I said."

I scoff. "Oh, yeah? Fuck this shit." I spin around, but before I can leave the room, Papa grabs my wrist.

"Sit down." His face is thunder black, his grip painfully tight. "And watch your fucking language."

"Let go!" I try to twist out of his hold, but he's too strong. Infuriated, I twist my arm harder, the adrenaline dulling the pain. "Let me fucking go!"

"Let her go. Now." Alexei's voice is dangerously level. It's the first time he's spoken today, and his words have the same effect as a judge's gavel banging in an unruly courtroom.

I freeze instinctively, and Papa drops my wrist as if it were a snake.

"Leave us," Alexei says, pushing to his feet to sweep an imperious gaze around the room. "Alina and I need to talk."

For half a beat, there's only silence. I don't expect any of the adults to obey, but to my shock, Boris Leonov stands up and my mom follows suit.

"We'll reconvene in ten," Papa says, his eyes narrowed on my face. "Behave, you hear me?"

With that, he strides out of the room, and Mama scurries after him. Boris is last. His dark gaze lingers on his son for a long moment, and then he departs too, leaving us alone in the library.

My knees suddenly feel wobbly, and I sink into the chair, rubbing my throbbing wrist. I'm shaking with adrenaline, my pulse hammering in my ears. I've never encountered this violent side of my father. I know it exists, but he's never hurt me before. Then again, I'd never outright defied him prior to today.

Alexei sits down as well and extends one hand toward me, palm up. "Let me see that," he orders.

Startled, I comply, showing him my wrist, where the skin is red and blotchy. To my shock, he gently takes my hand, a frown gathering between his eyebrows as he turns it this way and that. His touch jolts me with its warmth. His hand is dark against my pale skin, his fingers long and powerfully masculine.

My narrow palm and slender fingers look child-like in his grip. An electrifying tingle runs up my arm as he lightly rubs his thumb over the stinging skin, soothing the hurt, and my breathing quickens as the heated sensation spreads through my body, culminating in a pulsing, oddly pleasant ache between my thighs.

Oh, fuck. Is this what it feels like to be turned on? Is arousal what I've been experiencing around him?

I'm not ignorant about sex—we've had Sex Ed in school, and I've seen porn online—but I've never dated or had a boyfriend. Have never wanted to, no matter how much my friends make fun of me for finishing ninth grade without so much as kissing a boy. Natasha has already gone to third base with her boyfriend of six months, and a couple of my friends at school have had full-on sex. But I'm not ready. I don't want high school boys with their sloppy kisses and greedy caresses. Maybe it's because I've been gawked at by males of all ages since I turned twelve, but I've never been particularly eager to let anyone with a Y chromosome near me. I'm still not—but for the first time, I understand why other girls are.

If kissing is anything like the sensations Alexei's touch is evoking in my body, I might want to try it sooner rather than later.

But not with him. Never with him. Even if he hadn't killed my tutor, the Leonovs' reputation alone would make this a no-go.

I yank my arm back. "It's fine."

Alexei's gaze snaps up to my face. "It'll bruise."

"I'll put ice on it."

His expression smooths out. "As you wish. Now, let's talk about—"

"This insanity? Yeah, let's." I jump to my feet as fresh adrenaline floods my system. I don't care what kind of reaction I have to his touch or his nearness. I'm not marrying him, or anyone else my father picks for me.

My husband, if I ever have one, is going to be my choice and no one else's.

I begin pacing in front of the table. "This is total bullshit, and you need to tell them that. They seem to listen to you, so you have to speak up and say that it's not happening, that it's a ridiculous, barbaric thing they've come up with, and that neither of us wants it." I glance at Alexei and find his gaze tracking me with that indecipherable expression. "Right?"

He doesn't answer.

I stop, suddenly way less certain. "Right?"

"Sit," he says, gesturing to my chair. "There's something you need to know."

"What?"

He raises his eyebrows and gestures again.

Huffing, I plop into the damn chair. "What?"

"The betrothal agreement has already been signed."

"*What*? No. No, that's not true. They can't do it without us agreeing to it. They—" I stop at his sardonic smile. "They can?"

"Our families can do anything," he says softly. "You know that."

A chill spreads over my skin. He's right. I know he's

right. In Russia, the Molotovs and the Leonovs are close to omnipotent. Maybe if we were in the States or someplace like Germany, I could hope to find a judge or a police chief who hasn't been bought by one or both of our families, but not here in Moscow. Not anywhere in Eastern Europe, probably.

"Don't panic," Alexei says, correctly reading the expression on my face. "This isn't happening today or anytime soon. I have no interest in a fifteen-year-old, for marriage or for dating. For the foreseeable future, we'll carry on as we always have, leading our separate lives."

"Except we'll be betrothed." The very word is foreign on my tongue, as medieval as this whole arrangement.

"That's right." He regards me from underneath hooded eyelids.

"No, it's not right! Tell them to go fuck themselves." I can hear my voice rising, like that of a petulant child, so I clamp my lips shut. As much as I don't want this, the knowledge that he thinks of me as a dumb kid not even worth dating stings in some perverse way.

A sardonic curve touches his lips again. "You still don't understand. It's done. We *are* betrothed. Breaking the agreement now would only create fresh discord between our families. You don't want that, do you?"

I blink. "No, but—"

"Then we go along with it," he says with finality. "We take it one day at a time. Who knows where we'll be in a few years? Life isn't a static picture on a screen.

It changes all the time, in ways we can't even begin to predict. You can spend all your energy fighting the future today, or you can wait and see if a fight is worthwhile." He leans in, eyes gleaming. "In fact, when the time comes, you might find you've changed your mind about that future altogether."

Chapter 7

Present Day, Location Unknown

It's time you held up your end of our bargain.

Alexei's words reverberate through me, raising goosebumps all over my bare skin. Or maybe it's the warmth of his breath against my neck and the knowledge that I have nowhere to run, that after all these years, I'm finally going to lose this high-stakes game we've been playing. Then again, maybe it's for the best. I'm tired of running, tired of fighting.

I understand now that this man was always destined to destroy me.

It was written in the stars on the day both of us were born, precisely five years apart.

"That's it. Stop fighting it," he murmurs into my ear, loosening his grip on my wrists, and perversely, it's his words that provide me with the strength to resist the insidious desire thrumming inside me, the treacherous arousal weakening my knees. I may no longer be that naïve, foolishly brave fifteen-year-old, but a part of her is still within me.

With a jerky movement, I twist out of his hold and dart around him, backing up toward the middle of the spacious room. My heart hammers frantically, and it takes everything I have not to wrap my arms around my naked body, to stand tall as his eyes scorch a path over my bare breasts and belly before returning to my face.

His own face is drawn tight with savage need, spots of color burning hot on his high cheekbones. His voice is low and rough. "Is that how you wish to play it?"

I dampen my lips. "I'm hungry." It's a lie—I'm actually a little seasick—but it's the only thing I can think of to buy myself more time.

His nostrils flare, and I can sense the conflicting instincts warring inside him. In his own fucked-up way, he cares about me, about my comfort and well-being. He also wants me. He has ever since we first met, though I didn't know it until years later. My nails dig into my palms as I wait to see which side of him wins out.

He comes toward me, his steps slow and deliberate. "You're hungry."

I don't back away this time. What would be the point? I'm entirely at his mercy in this room, on this boat. My brothers are looking for me, I'm sure, but even with all the resources at their disposal, they won't find me anytime soon. A boat is nothing but a moving speck in a vast ocean.

Still, it's all I can do not to cringe away as he stops in front of me and tilts my chin up with curved fingers. I'm acutely cognizant of my nakedness, my vulnerability, especially since he's still dressed in the dark clothes he favors—not that he'd be any less intimidating without them. I'm above average in height, but he's at least a full head taller, his shoulders more than twice as broad as mine, his muscles cut from steel.

He can do anything he wants to me, and we both know it.

Fatalistically, I meet his coal-dark gaze and wait for him to decide my fate.

Chapter 8

8 Years and 5 Months Earlier, New Hampshire

SENIOR PROM, the shiny banner proclaims as I enter my high school gym, which has been transformed into a ballroom worthy of a palace. The latest pop songs blare from the speakers, and the atmosphere is thick with teenage hormones and drama. Occasionally, despite the chaperones' best efforts, you can also catch a whiff of pot.

I shouldn't be here, since I'm still a junior, but two of my best friends are seniors and they begged me to come with them, so here I am.

"You're our cute-guy bait," Risha told me. "We need you."

It's total bullshit, of course. An up-and-coming Bollywood star, Risha is as gorgeous as they come. She worries about me, though. So does our friend Giles. He thinks it's unnatural that I'm almost seventeen and haven't been on a single date.

"Do you think you might be asexual?" he asked me a

few months ago, his British accent lending the words a certain poshness. "It's totally cool if you are."

"I wish," I told him with a grimace. "Sadly, I like dick, same as you."

"Then why don't you get some?"

"I will. One day." When I'm no longer betrothed—but I couldn't tell him that. None of my friends at school know about the medieval contract hanging over my head, casting a shadow over every aspect of my life.

Even though I haven't seen Alexei since that day in my parents' library, I can't forget about him and the threat he poses to my future. I dread each birthday because even though no actual dates have been set, I know that eighteen is most likely when I'll be deemed "old enough." At least for dating, if not for marriage—and I can only guess what dating a man like Alexei Leonov will entail.

I fought against the betrothal, of course. No matter what Alexei said, I couldn't meekly accept the situation and wait to see how it shakes out in the future. For three days straight, I cried and begged; for months afterward, I gave my parents the silent treatment. Time and time again, I told them I won't do it and they can't make me. None of it mattered. The contract stands, and even though Alexei isn't in my life yet, I know he will be soon.

"There you are," Risha yells, spotting me from the dance floor. She waves madly. "Come join us!"

I wave back. "I'm getting a drink first!"

Pushing through the crowds, I make my way to the

refreshments station. There's punch, naturally, but there's also sparkling water, sparkling grape juice, kombucha, and every non-alcoholic cocktail you can imagine, prepared by an actual bartender.

When rich kids party, you can't get by with something as basic as colored sugar water.

I get a glass of kombucha, because microbiome, and then I discreetly bum a joint off of a guy I know. In the past year, I've discovered that I like pot. It quiets the anxiety that always gnaws at my stomach these days.

I'm on my way to the bathroom to sneak in a quick smoke when a tall figure steps in front of me.

"Hey there."

Ugh, this again. "Hey, Josh," I say with an eyeroll.

I knew he'd be here—everybody expects him to be voted Prom King—but I was hoping he'd be too busy with his girlfriend to hit on me. But no. He's found the time.

"You here with someone or by yourself?" he drawls, running a hand through his long-ish blond hair—undoubtedly to draw my attention to how smooth and shiny it is. His gaze travels over my body from the tips of my silver heels to the spaghetti straps holding up my Givenchy dress, and the look in his blue eyes makes me want to pull my bodice higher.

Gamely, I resist the urge. "I'm with my friends."

"Oh, yeah?" He leans in, smirking. "How about I show you around?"

"No, thanks. I've got to drain the lady lizard." There. If that doesn't cool his ardor, I don't know what will.

Before he can come up with a response, I step around him and beeline for the bathroom. It's still early in the evening, so it's not yet swarmed by all the girls surreptitiously adding alcohol to their virgin cocktails. I find an empty stall and light up, enjoying the acrid, grassy burn in my throat as the smoke travels deep into my lungs. Almost immediately, the anxious buzzing of my thoughts quiets down, the tension gripping my temples easing. Another drag, and my mind empties further. For a few blessed moments, I forget that the school year will be over soon and I'll have to go home to Moscow, to my parents' ever-escalating fights… that this summer, I'll turn seventeen, one year closer to the age I dread and the man I fear.

What makes it worse is that I'm sure Alexei hasn't given me or the stupid contract a moment's thought since that day. I have neither seen him nor heard from him in almost two years, and he's certainly made no attempt to get to know me. Which is good. Hopefully, he's forgotten all about me by now, and when the time comes, he *will* tell our fathers to go fuck themselves.

I should find that thought reassuring—and I do—but sometimes, my imagination plays tricks on me. Sometimes, I could swear I feel his presence nearby, as if he were a ghost hovering over me, watching me. Worse yet, each time I'm tempted to say "yes" when a boy asks me out, I remember Dan's ring, and a "no" leaves my lips instead.

Would Alexei know if I dated someone at my school? And if he did, would he care?

I'd like to think that he wouldn't, but I can't risk it.

I can't be responsible for another person disappearing because of me.

A few more drags, and I'm done with the joint. My head feels both heavy and light, my thoughts disjointed in the way only pot or a lot of alcohol can achieve. I'm not a fan of the latter because of my father, but I like getting high. I like this feeling of not being all there.

Sometimes, when my parents' fights get especially brutal, I wonder what it would be like to not be there at all.

Pushing open the door of the stall, I come out, wash my hands, and make sure my makeup is in place. Then I make my way to the dance floor, where I find Risha and Giles grinding against their respective crushes.

Of course. I should've known that this whole "come with us, we need company because we don't have dates" business was just a ploy to get me here. They're probably hoping that I'll get a little drunk, a little high, and next thing you know, I'll be making out with some football player in the back of his daddy's limo.

Yeah, nice try, guys.

I am a little high, though—okay, more than a little —so I let myself get dragged into the throng of gyrating bodies. With my mind all hazy, the beat of the music feels seductive, the pulsing tempo reminding me of the sensations I feel when I wake up from one of those nightmares about Alexei and press my hand to the empty ache between my legs. If I press hard enough and rub for a while, the sensations grow and crest until they're too sweet, too sharp. That's when I back off.

I back off because as I approach that peak, I see his face and I forget why belonging to him would be a terrible idea.

The music changes, a new song coming on. It's one of my favorites. I close my eyes, letting the autotuned words wash over me as the familiar beat guides the movements of my body. Somebody starts grinding up on me from behind, their hands skimming over my bare arms before clasping my hips to pull my ass against a growing male bulge. A guy then. I can feel his warmth. He's breathing hard, sweating, but for once, I'm not repelled. I'm floating in the haze veiling my mind, letting the hypnotic beat sweep me away.

"Yeah, go, Alina!" Risha's excited voice reaches me over the music, and I laugh, suddenly giddy. Why haven't I done this before? Why have I shut myself away to live like a nun, all because of some ridiculous, unenforceable piece of paper?

I'm not betrothed.

I refuse to be.

"Shake it, girl," Giles shouts, and I do. It's like something has broken loose inside me. I have no idea who's grinding up on me, but I don't care. It's not about some boy. It's about me. Swaying my hips to the music, I open my eyes, and the multicolored strobe lights overhead mix with the fog from the machines, adding to the surreal feeling engulfing me. I'm no longer myself. I'm someone else, someone I don't recognize. Someone wild and free.

The guy behind me grinds up on me harder. He grows bolder, moving his hands from my hips to my ribs and then higher, higher… "Fuck!" he exclaims, stiffening suddenly, and to my dismay, I recognize Josh's voice. Before I can react, I'm spun around and dragged off the dance floor by a strong hand wrapped around my upper arm.

I'm so stunned and disoriented that I don't struggle at first. And by the time I do, I'm already in a dark corner of the gym away from the crowds, shielded from view by a stack of bleachers covered by decorative banners. A tall, broad figure in a tuxedo looms over me.

"What—" I begin, blinking, only to freeze in shock as I recognize the dark eyes and the hard features of the man in front of me.

Alexei Leonov.

My intended.

And he is furious.

His voice is a low, dark snarl. "What the fuck do you think you're doing?"

"What?" I struggle to wrangle my disjointed thoughts into some semblance of coherence. Is this for real, or have I smoked way too much? There's no way Alexei is here, at my high school prom. *In New Hampshire.*

He lets go of my arm and grips my jaw in one big hand to turn my face one way, then the other, peering into my eyes intently the whole time. "You're fucking high." He sounds both disgusted and disbelieving.

"Um, yeah." Wait, should I have denied it? Fuck. This is real. But how? Why? What is he doing here? It occurs to me that I should probably ask that last bit out loud. "What are you doing here?"

There. I sound almost normal. Except I'm not. I'm high as fuck, and nothing about this situation is normal. I was dancing with Josh—yuck—and then… Oh, shit. The adrenaline clears away some of the fog in my brain, and horror floods in as Alexei tightens his grip on my jaw, squeezing my cheeks into a pout, and bends his head over me, his eyes burning like live coals.

"You do not fucking dance with other men." Each word falls on my ears like an executioner's axe. "You do not look at them—and you do not, under any fucking circumstances, let them touch you. Contractually and in every other way, you are mine. Understand?"

I'm so stunned I can only blink in answer. It must not be enough because he brings his face closer, until our noses are barely three inches apart. His nostrils flare dangerously. "Say you fucking understand."

With the way he's holding my jaw, I can't say anything, so I just make an "uh-huh" noise in the back of my throat. I can feel the repressed violence within him, the fury that's on the verge of boiling over, and my heartbeat skyrockets, clearing more of the haze in my brain.

This isn't a nightmare or my imagination playing tricks. It's happening. He's here, in the flesh.

Contrary to my hopes, he hasn't forgotten me.

My latest attempt at an answer must mollify him because his grip on my face gentles slightly. However, he doesn't release me, nor does he move his face away. Instead, his gaze falls on my lips, still pouted by his fingers squeezing my cheeks, and a different sort of tension invades his powerful body. I can feel it, the heat rising off his skin, the way his breathing grows heavier, more uneven. My own breath shallows out in response, a warm lassitude sweeping through me, weakening my knees and liquifying my core. Every dream, every nightmare I've ever had about him, is suddenly vivid in my mind, as are those sweet, sharp sensations that I refuse to take to their natural conclusion. Because *he* is responsible for them. He's the only one who's ever made me feel this way.

"Were you going to let him kiss you?" His voice is rough as he brings his head down until his mouth hovers just above mine, his breath warm and cinnamon-flavored against my lips. "Were you going to let him fuck you?"

"N-no." I don't really know what I'm saying. I'd say anything to feel his lips on mine. I'm trembling with the force of my need, my heart thundering so loudly it's all I can hear. My first kiss. I never knew it was possible to want something so badly. And he wants it too. He must. Surely, any second now he'll—

He drops his hand and steps back with a suddenness that jolts me. "Good. Don't." His tone is shockingly cold and hard. "You are my betrothed, and I don't share. Ever."

With that, he turns and walks away, leaving me shaken to the core. I don't see him or Josh again for the remainder of the night.

In fact, I don't see Josh ever again, and neither does anyone else.

Like my tutor, he simply disappears.

Chapter 9

Present Day, Location Unknown

Alexei's eyes are midnight black as he stares down at me, his jaw flexing, and as the silence between us stretches, I'm certain his base desires will win out. But I'm wrong. He lets me go and steps back, dropping his hand.

"Let's feed you then," he says, his dry tone telling me he knows it's just another stalling tactic on my part.

I don't care, though. I've won myself more time. "I need clothes," I say, proud of how calm I sound. "Where can I—"

He gestures to a sliding door. "That closet has everything you need."

Okay, so he doesn't plan to keep me naked. Yay. Sometimes, you have to celebrate the little things.

I hurry to the closet before he changes his mind. My face burns as I feel his eyes on my naked backside. My ass is nicely toned—I've done lots of hiking and gym workouts in recent months—yet I can't help but wonder if he's seen better. Touched better. I have no reason to think he's been as faithful to me as I've been forced to be to him.

It's a thought that, as always, fills my veins with acid.

Suppressing it, I push the sliding door aside and step into a walk-in closet that's nearly as large as what I had at Nikolai's compound, though neither is comparable to the spacious room that houses my clothes and accessories in Moscow. Nonetheless, the selection here is pretty solid. I find dresses and heels by many of my favorite designers, along with about a million swimsuits, casual sundresses, shorts, T-shirts, and a wide selection of flat sandals and flip-flops.

It's tempting to put on something casual and comfy, but I reach for a cocktail dress instead. Made of heavy green silk with a fitted sweetheart bodice and flared knee-length skirt, it's going to make me look and feel put-together. More in control.

It's something I badly need right now.

I find appropriate underwear—a strapless green bra and matching thong—in a built-in drawer in the corner and quickly dress. A pair of nude heels completes the look.

When I step out, Alexei is looking out a window, his hands interlaced behind his back. Hearing my footsteps, he turns and gives me a slow once-over, his eyes dragging a burning path over my body. "Beautiful, as always."

I've heard a version of this compliment a thousand

times, yet the huskily uttered words sound different coming from him. Darker. Scarier. There's a possessiveness in his tone that chills me. He's not looking at me with appreciation, but with satisfaction, the kind that the owner of an expensive painting might express when viewing it hanging on his wall.

And that's basically what I am to him. A possession. A trophy he's finally ready to hang on his wall.

A trophy he's won by slaughtering dozens this week alone.

"Thank you," I reply coolly, suppressing a shudder. "Now, where will we eat?"

A mocking smile curves his lips as he holds his hand out in an unmistakable invitation. "Come, I'll show you."

It's a test, a challenge. He's daring me to resist, to fight him on this small thing so he'll have an excuse to do his worst. Well, he's out of luck. I hold my head high as I approach and place my palm in his. My heart jumps into my throat as his strong fingers close around mine, his grip warm and electrifying, but I keep my face carefully blank, not letting him see how his touch affects me as he leads me out of the room.

Outside is a hallway about four feet wide with several more doors on either side of it. Straight ahead is a spiral staircase. As we head toward it, I walk carefully, the swaying of the boat underneath making me feel like I'm wearing high heels for the first time.

That's probably why there's such a big selection of

flat shoes in my closet. If the seas get any rockier, I'll need them.

Steadying me by the elbow, Alexei leads me up the stairs. We emerge onto a long, wide deck. The sun blinds me for a moment—I should've grabbed a pair of sunglasses from the closet—but he guides me under an overhang that provides shade, and my eyes adjust enough to take in our surroundings.

As I suspected, we're in the open ocean. Dark blue water surrounds us, stretching as far as the eye can see. Above us, near the bow of the boat, is another deck, a smaller one. We're on a yacht, it looks like, one that's big and luxurious but not outrageously so. That's smart of him. If my brothers think to look for a boat, this one is less likely to blip on their radar than a seven-hundred-million-dollar superyacht.

Deeper under the overhang is a round, tablecloth-covered table with two place settings and two chairs. Alexei leads me to it and pulls out a chair for me—a gentlemanly gesture that belies the truth of our situation. The sardonic tilt of his lips tells me he knows that.

"Thank you," I say. Because why not? If he wants to play gracious host after violently kidnapping and drugging me, who am I to stop him? Sitting down gracefully, I pick up a neatly folded white cloth napkin from the table and spread it over my lap, as if we were on a date at a nice restaurant. In the meantime, he walks around and takes the other seat.

Footsteps sound to the left of me, and I turn my head to see a man approaching. Tall, lean, and white-haired, he's dressed in a white-and-blue uniform and boasts the deeply tanned, leathery complexion of someone who spends most of his life outdoors. Reaching the table, the newcomer takes off his cap and executes a bow. "Miss Molotova, it's a pleasure to meet you."

I hide my surprise at being addressed in American English. I figured Alexei's goons would be Russian.

"I'm Jack Larson, captain of this vessel," the man continues. "If there's anything you need, please don't hesitate to ask."

"Thank you, Larson," Alexei says before I can reply. Though he didn't study in the States, his English is as unaccented as mine. "Please tell Vika we're ready for lunch."

Lunch? I squint at the bright sun. Does that mean it's around noon? Exactly where are we? How long has it been since he stole me from Nikolai's compound in Idaho?

Larson bows again. "Yes, sir." He strides away, leaving me alone with Alexei.

"You never told me where we are," I say as soon as Larson's footsteps fade. "What is this body of water?"

Alexei's grin is sharp and white. "What does it matter? It's not like you'll be able to contact anyone to tell them."

"Exactly. So why not tell me?"

He shrugs infuriatingly. "Why tell you?"

I grit my teeth. "Maybe because it's common courtesy when you kidnap someone?"

"I didn't kidnap you." His eyes harden. "You came with me willingly, remember? Just yesterday, you said, and I quote, 'I will come with you. I will honor the betrothal contract.' Unless that promise was also a lie?"

I drag in an unsteady breath, my hands scrunching the tablecloth on either side of my place setting. How dare he try to twist this around, to make *me* the villain in our fucked-up story? "I didn't lie to you. You know I never wanted this."

He leans in, trapping my hands underneath his. "Liar," he says softly. His eyes glow a fierce black. "Even now, you're lying to me—and to yourself. You wanted me before you even turned fourteen, and you sure as fuck wanted me when you were eighteen. And you want me still, no matter how hard you try to run from it. But guess what?" His hands tighten over mine, his voice roughening as his eyes burn into me. "You have nowhere to run now, nowhere to hide. Before this day is over, Alinyonok, you *will* face the truth. You will know that you are, and always have been, mine."

Chapter 10

7 Years and 2 Months Earlier, Moscow

My eighteenth birthday.

I feel sick to my stomach just thinking about it. My parents are throwing a huge party tonight, one that will be attended by everybody who's anybody in Moscow. My mom has been in planning mode for months, wanting it to be *the* event of the summer. The celebration will take place in a huge ballroom at the newest luxury hotel, and the worst part is that I overheard my parents arguing over whether to announce my engagement to Alexei there.

"—haven't even dated yet," Mama was saying in a shrill tone when I walked past the library a few days ago. "What if they don't like each other? What if he refuses at the last moment? He hasn't so much as spoken to her in years!"

"Because she was a fucking child," Papa retorted sharply. "He said he wouldn't come near her until she was older, and he hasn't. But she's eighteen now. What the fuck is there to wait for? Boris is on board."

"What about our daughter, you selfish monster? You don't think *she* should be on board as well?"

"What the fuck does she know about what she wants? She got into Columbia, and what does she want to study there? Fucking computer bullshit. Like we need another social retard in the family."

"Don't you talk about Kostya that way!"

"He's my fucking son, and I'll talk about him whichever fucking way I want!"

A crash accompanied the words—a chair flying, most likely—and I couldn't stand to listen any longer. I escaped to my room, where I retreated into a video game for hours. But it wasn't enough to keep my stomach from roiling and my head from feeling like little hammers were pounding my brain. The headaches I used to fake have become all too real over the past year, assaulting me at random times. Or maybe not so random—they come whenever I think about my parents and the future that awaits me with Alexei.

A future that holds a marriage that I'm increasingly convinced will be as big of a disaster as my parents'.

Last week, I saw a bruise on Mama's arm. A big, ugly one. She said she'd bumped into a kitchen cabinet, but I have my doubts. Papa has been drinking extra heavily this summer, and I feel like he's not in control of himself half the time. I told Konstantin, and he said he's been trying to convince Mama to leave, to finally divorce Papa. She assured Konstantin that she's thinking about it, but I have my doubts on that front also.

Even now, as their mutual loathing poisons the very air around them, my parents seem pulled to each other, chained together by some unholy force that supersedes simple labels like love or hate. They're toxic together, but they seem unable to be apart.

A throbbing pain assaults my temples anew, adding to the queasiness in my stomach. It makes me want to crawl into my bed and draw the covers over my head, to shut out the world completely. But I can't. I have to get ready for the party.

Swallowing against the nausea, I open a bottle of Excedrin and down two pills with a glass of water. The pills rarely help, but they're better than nothing. I have an appointment with my parents' doctor next week. Hopefully, he'll prescribe me something stronger. In the meantime, maybe I'll score some pot at the party. It's not a cure-all, but it helps more than Excedrin.

A knock on my door catches my attention. It's followed by a tentative, "Alina? Pavel would like to know if you're hungry."

Ugh, great. It's Lyudmila, Natasha's former housekeeper. She's been working for us ever since she and Pavel got married, and she is not my favorite person. Nikolai and Valery think it's because I have some kind of weird daddy crush on Pavel, but they're wrong.

It's because I haven't forgiven her for her role in my parents finding out about Dan's ring and Alexei's note.

Maybe it's unfair to blame her for the betrothal, but I can't help thinking that if my father hadn't learned about Alexei's involvement in my tutor's disappearance, he wouldn't have come up with the idea to unite our families in this barbaric manner. Without Lyudmila ratting me out, he wouldn't have known that Alexei had any interest in me, and the whole thing might not have come to pass.

"I'm not hungry," I call out, unable to hide the irritation in my voice. The raging headache isn't helping my mood. "I'm getting ready for the party."

"Of course," Lyudmila replies quickly. "I'll let him know."

Her footsteps fade away, and I feel a pang of guilt. Blabbermouth or not, Lyudmila doesn't deserve my attitude. I should try to be nicer, if only for Pavel's sake. I know he loves her, and she seems to love him. And unlike my parents' toxic marriage, theirs seems to be a simple, straightforward union, even though Pavel shares my father's ruthlessness and propensity for violence.

It almost makes me believe it's possible to find happiness with a dangerous man—"almost" being the operative word.

Lost in these ruminations, I dress, arrange my hair into a sleek updo, and apply makeup on autopilot. By the time I'm done, the headache has let up slightly, and it's time to drive over to the hotel. Mama is already there, overseeing the catering and everything else, and

Papa is heading there straight from a business meeting, so I'm going with my brothers.

Konstantin and Valery are waiting in the living room when I come downstairs, and Nikolai is due to arrive any second. I don't know why Mama decided I need all three of them to escort me—or anyone other than our bodyguards, really—but I don't mind. I rarely get to see my brothers, especially all together like this. We each attended—or currently attend—different boarding schools and universities abroad, and all three of my brothers have served in the army at various points in recent years. Valery is still not done with his service, in fact; he's just here for my birthday celebration.

I smile as he stands up from the couch to greet me. "How's the army life treating you?"

He bends down to kiss my cheek as befits a good brother, but when he steps back, his answering smile doesn't reach his cool amber-green eyes. "As well as can be expected." He runs his gaze over me. "You look nice. Parents will be pleased."

Yes, they will be. I wonder why he said that, though. If he were anyone else, I'd dismiss it as an innocent compliment, but you can't do that with Valery. He doesn't say or do anything without some hidden agenda. It's been that way for as long as I can remember.

Though he's the closest to me in age, being only twenty, Valery is the brother I know and understand the least. Even Nikolai, who shares way too many of our father's traits, is more comprehensible to me. With Valery, it's all about nuances and layers, hidden meanings and covert agendas.

It's exhausting, frankly.

"We should get going," Konstantin says as he looks up from his phone screen and rises from the couch. As usual, he's oblivious to the need for any sort of greeting. "The traffic will delay us by fifteen and a half minutes."

I grin up at him. Fifteen and a half, of course. That's Kostya for you. If he could, he'd quantify and digitize every aspect of our lives, turn everything into zeros and ones. Papa hates that about him, always has, but I think it's what makes my oldest brother so brilliant. Nikolai and Valery appreciate his abilities too. Unlike our father, who's still caught up in the nineties' mentality of might-makes-right, they understand the importance of technology to our future. It will be Konstantin's dark web ventures and the like that will grow our family's power and influence in the coming years, not our real estate assets or oil-and-gas fields.

Then again, what do I know? According to my parents, the only way I can contribute to our family's fortune is by looking pretty and marrying Alexei.

My mood darkens at the thought, and it's all I can do to keep my smile as Nikolai enters the room and also greets me with a kiss on the cheek. When he pulls back, his lips are curved in one of his signature ovary-slaying smiles. All three of my brothers are strikingly handsome and look enough alike to be triplets, but

Nikolai—or Kolya, as I've called him since childhood—possesses that certain extra something. Animal magnetism, maybe? Personally, I don't feel it, but women are drawn to him like sugar ants to bait. Unfortunately for them, he just toys with them for a night or two and then discards them, broken-hearted. On second thought, maybe I should say "fortunately."

Underneath that beautiful exterior, he's as dark and intensely obsessive as our father, and I'd pity any woman he truly fixated on.

"My limo is waiting outside," he says, offering me his arm. "Let's get our Cinderella to her ball."

"If only I had the option to meet Prince Charming there," I mutter under my breath as I slip my arm through the crook of his elbow.

Nikolai hears me anyway. He shoots me a sharp look as he leads me to the door that opens into the elevator foyer. "You know our parents are hoping to announce the engagement tonight, right?"

Some of my nausea returns. "I overheard something to that effect, yes."

Valery falls into step beside us. "I can talk to them if that's not what you want. Get them to pump the brakes for now." His tone is cool, emotionless, but the stare he levels at me is unnervingly penetrating.

My heart leaps with hope. "You can?"

He nods, as if it's no big deal, and Nikolai says, "I'll back him up. You're way too young for marriage. Especially with a Leonov." He imbues the last word with derision.

"Actually, I've already spoken with our father," Konstantin says from behind us. We all stop and turn to look at him, surprised. He calmly adjusts his glasses, unruffled by the attention. "He's agreed that the timing of the announcement and everything else that follows should be up to Alina and Alexei from now on. As long as the betrothal agreement remains in place, they can decide how to proceed from here."

My mouth drops open, and I'm not the only one with that reaction. I have some idea of how Valery would have achieved his goal—he can outwit and out-manipulate anyone, our father included—and I wouldn't have been surprised if Nikolai, as the favored heir, would've exerted a fair amount of influence as well. But Konstantin? How on Earth did he do this? Papa has despised him ever since he was a toddler, when it became clear that he was different from other kids and had zero interest in learning what Papa had to teach him.

"Kostya..." My voice is uneven, the tips of my fingers icy as I curl them against my palms. "Are you sure? Could you have misunderstood, maybe?"

He cocks his head, considering it. "No," he says after a long moment, during which my emotions oscillate wildly, bouncing between hope and dread. "Father was quite clear. He understood the alternative."

My breath whooshes out in relief as Valery asks, "What alternative?"

Out of the three of us, he looks the least surprised by this development. It makes me wonder if this was part of his backup plan. Because Valery always has a backup plan. And a backup to the backup plan.

Konstantin pulls out his phone and glances at the screen again. "We have seventy-three seconds of leeway with the current state of traffic. If we don't get moving, we'll be late."

I'm dying to interrogate him further, and I'm sure Nikolai and Valery are too, but he's right. We have to get going, or we won't make it to the party on time—a party that I'm suddenly dreading way less.

If Konstantin is telling the truth, and I have no reason to think he's not, tonight doesn't have to spell my doom.

My thoughts spin madly as we get into the elevator and descend to the underground parking garage where Nikolai's limo awaits. I have a million questions for my oldest brother, but I know better than to ask them outside the privacy of our penthouse, where our security team performs daily sweeps for listening devices and such. This is a private elevator, one that goes up only to our penthouse, but still, it's less secure. Whichever levers Konstantin used to convince Papa to back off are, most likely, things our enemies can use against us. Now that the initial shock is fading, I can think of several ways Konstantin might've strong-armed our father into doing what he wants, and they all have to do with what Papa thinks of as Konstantin's weakness: his all-consuming passion for computers and technology.

With Konstantin's hacking abilities and intimate

knowledge of our family's business, it's all too easy to imagine him taking an important factory offline with a few strokes on his keyboard, or freezing our liquid assets in the Cayman Islands. Or making them disappear altogether.

In his own quiet way, Konstantin might be the most dangerous of my three brothers.

Finally, we're in the limo, and as soon as the partition between us and Nikolai's driver goes up, I can't hold back any longer. Turning to Konstantin, I begin, "So, Kostya, how did you—"

"You still need to talk to Alexei," he says, and I forget all about his Papa-handling methodology as he continues. "Father won't force the issue, but the Leonovs may insist that the announcement proceeds as planned."

My chest feels like a balloon that's just been punctured. The hope that buoyed me a second ago bleeds out, taking with it most of the air in my lungs. I somehow missed that part the first time, where he said that Papa agreed to leave it up to me and *Alexei.*

Not just me.

I have to get *him* on board as well.

All the anxiety I've been battling returns, multiplied tenfold, and my temples throb anew. *Talk to Alexei.* This, more than anything, is the reason I've been losing sleep over this party.

Because *he'll* be there.

I haven't seen him since my junior-year prom, but I know he's been around, watching me. That feeling of a ghostly presence hovering over me, the feeling I dismissed before that fateful dance, is with me all the time. Somehow, he's keeping tabs on me, ever ready to swoop in if I step a foot out of line. I don't know if he truly wants me or if he's acting on some bizarre territorial instinct, but I haven't so much as smiled at a member of the opposite sex since that night. I don't dare.

Two deaths on my conscience is plenty.

All of my friends are convinced I'm either asexual or a closet lesbian, but they couldn't be more wrong. I want sexual intimacy with a man. I crave it. Half the time, when I wake up in the morning, it's with the sheets tangled around my legs and my hands pressing between my thighs in a futile effort to quench the ache pulsing deep inside.

I'm eighteen and I've never been kissed, never been touched outside of that brief dance with poor Josh—may his remains rest in peace wherever they are.

"*I* can talk to Alexei," Nikolai says, his jaw set dangerously. "There's no reason for her to deal with that asshole. He'll back down. I'll make him."

"Not a good idea," Valery says, as icy calm as always. "He hates all three of us and will press ahead with the announcement just to spite us. We'll need serious leverage before we bring it up with him." He looks at our oldest brother. "Konstantin, maybe you can—"

"It's fine," I say and take a breath. "I'll talk to Alexei myself."

As much as I want to let my brothers fight my

battle, I know Valery is right. There's bad blood between our families, always has been, and it wouldn't take more than a spark to blow apart the fragile rapport Papa has established with Boris Leonov. Not that I care about Papa's agenda or anything along those lines. I'm just worried that if Nikolai or Valery try to strong-arm Alexei with Konstantin's help, it could backfire, and instead of the betrothal announcement getting postponed, I might find myself stolen away and married tomorrow.

The Leonovs are capable of anything and everything.

"Are you sure?" Konstantin asks, frowning at me. "He's—"

"It's fine." It's not—nothing about this is fine—but I don't want my brothers dragged into my mess. At least not if I can handle it myself by growing some balls.

So what if Alexei is the man who haunts my dreams and nightmares? The one I can't help thinking about each time I bring myself to the very edge of ecstasy, only to back off? I can still talk to him, make him see reason. No matter how he acted the night of that dance, he probably doesn't want to be betrothed to me either and would welcome the opportunity to postpone the announcement indefinitely—if I approach him the right way.

"All right," Nikolai says. "But let us know if he's being difficult."

"Don't worry." I smooth my damp palms over my

dress and lift my chin, ignoring the heavy pounding of my heart. "I've got this."

After all, I'm a Molotov as well.

The party is everything my parents hoped it would be—a spectacle so over-the-top it'll be talked about in Moscow for years to come. The glitterati have turned out in full force. In addition to high-ranking government officials and local business moguls, attendees include international movie stars and supermodels, American tech billionaires, Italian fashion designers, and famous artists of all kinds. Every female's neck and earlobes sport jewelry pieces worth more than most people's houses, and the glamorous gowns and tuxedos filling the giant ballroom easily top what's seen and drooled over at the Oscars. The entertainment is equally impressive. A famous Russian band is performing live throughout the night, and at midnight, Beyoncé will appear to sing one of her hits, followed by several other international pop stars. There will also be a dance performed by Bolshoi Ballet and an hour-long aerial acrobatics show by Cirque du Soleil.

Under other circumstances, I'd enjoy all of it, but with the conversation with Alexei hanging over my head, it's all I can do to smile, shake hands, and exchange air kisses with the well-wishers. It seems as if everyone wants to talk to me, to comment on my gown, my jewelry, my looks. I field joking and not-so-joking inquiries about my dating life from friends and strangers alike—apparently, everybody thinks I should be paired up by now—and answer all sorts of probing questions about my post-graduation plans.

Why, yes, I'm starting at Columbia this fall. No, I didn't consider a university in Paris. Thank you, but I have no interest in Fashion Design as a major. Economics and PoliSci, like Nikolai? No, that's not really my cup of tea either. I'm more interested in Computer Science, like Konstantin.

Even as I say all this, I can't help wondering if any of it is true. Am I starting at Columbia in a few weeks? Will I be able to study what I want? Live in New York City like I want? Because there's a very real chance all of my plans are about to crash and burn. I've been making decisions about my future as if the betrothal contract didn't exist and my life were my own, but that's not the case. On paper, I belong to Alexei, and he could insist I attend a university in Moscow to be closer to him, or even not go to college at all. Of course, I have no intention of letting him dictate my life, but if my parents don't side with me—and they've given zero indication that they would—it would be difficult, if not impossible, to make Columbia happen.

It's yet another reason I need to talk to Alexei tonight. I need to know where he stands on this cursed betrothal, if he's as opposed to it as I hope he is. After all, he's young too, only twenty-three to my eighteen. What guy that age wants marriage? Or even the promise of it? True, Alexei is no ordinary twenty-something—rumor has it, he's been running the Leonov organization behind the scenes for the past couple of years—but I bet he still likes to party and wouldn't want a fiancée (or worse, a wife) cramping his style.

In fact, he might have some beauty warming his bed as we speak, helping him celebrate *his* birthday tonight.

My stomach twists peculiarly at the thought, and I escape the crowd with an excuse about needing to use the bathroom. As much as I dread the upcoming confrontation with Alexei, it bothers me that I haven't spotted him at the party yet. It's still early in the evening, but he *is* my fucking betrothed. Shouldn't he have been one of the first to wish me a happy birthday? Not that I want him to, but it would've been the polite, civilized thing to do. Then again, what do the Leonovs know about politeness and civilized behavior?

They're savages, always have been.

I use the restroom and wash my hands before drying them on a soft towel offered by a uniformed bathroom attendant. To my relief, the floor-to-ceiling mirror behind the modern-artsy floating sink reflects a young woman who's all gloss and glitter, her cool smile hiding the turmoil within. Nobody looking at me would guess that I'm a nervous wreck with a rapidly intensifying headache, or that all I want is to return home to my room and fall asleep after sneaking a few desperately needed puffs.

Speaking of which… I exit the women's restroom

and make my way across the hall to the men's. As I hoped, Vova is skulking by the entrance there, looking all fancy in his tailored tux and not at all like the high-end weed dealer that he is.

"The usual?" he asks at my approach, and I nod, passing him a couple of bills from my tiny purse in exchange for a rolled-up, fully prepped joint.

"You sure you don't want something stronger?" he asks as I'm about to turn away. "I've got a few special treats tonight."

I shouldn't. I know I shouldn't, but my right temple feels like it's getting drilled by an unlicensed dentist. "Like what?"

Vova's smile makes him look like the Cheshire cat. "Molly, coke, a few other party accessories."

I wrinkle my nose. "No, thanks."

"How about some painkillers?" He opens his palm to show me a couple of white pills. "It's good, strong shit, but my grandmother no longer needs it. She passed away last week."

"I'm sorry to hear that."

He shrugs as I stare at the pills, debating. I haven't tried this sort of thing before, but if it's for pain, shouldn't it help the hammers dancing in my skull? And dull the anxiety twisting me up inside? Maybe it's exactly what my parents' doctor will prescribe me next week. Before I can talk myself out of it, I snatch up the two pills and dry-swallow them.

"Whoa there," Vova says with a laugh as I plop three

more bills onto his palm in payment. "One is the starter dose."

Dammit. Now I might be high instead of headache-free. Oh, well. Maybe it'll make this party more tolerable.

Leaving Vova to his skulking, I return to the ballroom, where I'm immediately surrounded by a group of friends, acquaintances, and people I've previously seen only on TV and in society gossip rags. Everybody wants to suck up to the birthday girl, and before I know it, it's an hour later and my headache is a distant memory. In its place is a fuzzy glow that softens the edges of reality and makes me feel like I'm observing everyone and everything from a small distance.

I like it. A lot. These pills are even better than pot at taming my anxiety. I'm so calm I'm practically catatonic.

I'm on my way to the restrooms to ask Vova if he has any more pills for me to buy when a tall, broad-shouldered man steps in front of me, blocking my path. Startled, I look up—and my stomach performs a somersault that would make Cirque du Soleil proud.

Alexei.

He's finally here.

"Happy birthday," he says, his deep voice audible despite the music and the din of the hundred different conversations around us. His dark eyes gleam as he gives me a slow once-over. "You look beautiful, as always."

All of my calm flees. My heart does a loopy lurch inside my chest, even as the fuzziness at the edges of my vision intensifies. "Thank you," I say breathlessly. "Happy birthday to you too. I hope you've had a chance to celebrate it?"

Fuck, I hope I'm making sense. I've never felt like this before, completely out of it, yet on edge. My heart is racing madly, my palms are sweating, and my eyes can't stop scouring his face, his body… every strong, vital inch of him. Is it possible he's grown even harder, more intimidating, in the fifteen months since my prom?

Twenty-three or not, the powerful, self-assured man in front of me seems more than capable of ruling a dark empire—or the Leonov organization, which is one and the same.

"I'm still celebrating it," he says as his eyes travel over me again, raising goosebumps on my arms and making heat ignite under my skin. "The night is not over yet. And in twenty minutes, we'll have another reason to celebrate."

I blink up at him, my brain operating maddeningly slowly. It takes me a moment to realize he must be referring to the engagement announcement—the very reason I need to talk to him ASAP. I'm about to blurt exactly that when he reaches into his jacket's inner pocket and takes out a small black velvet box.

The words freeze on my lips as my lungs cease to function. Paralyzed by horror, I stare at the box as my mind flashes back to the other such box he gave me, the one that held Dan's ring. Frantically, I try to think if there's someone else, some other man in my life who could've given Alexei the erroneous impression that—

He pops the box open with a casual flick of his thumb, revealing a gorgeous princess-cut diamond surrounded by emeralds. Set in a delicate, diamond-encrusted platinum circle, it's unmistakably a woman's ring… and exactly what I would've wanted for my engagement, if I'd wanted the latter at all.

I should feel relieved that it's not another gruesome gift of the kind a cat might bring to its owner, but a different kind of horror grabs hold of me as Alexei orders softly, "Give me your hand," and takes out the ring, slipping the box back into his pocket. Frozen, I watch as he clasps my left hand in his and slides the ring onto my finger, leaving no doubt of what this gift is supposed to signify.

Possession. Ownership.

The end of my freedom.

No. No, no, no.

I don't even realize I'm saying the word out loud until Alexei's hand tightens painfully around mine.

"What the fuck do you mean, no?" His voice is low and dangerous, his jaw set in a harsh line. "You are my fiancée."

I yank my hand out of his grasp. "No, I'm not!"

Faces turn toward us, eyes wide with curiosity. I must've spoken louder than I thought.

Alexei's face darkens further, and with a sinking feeling, I realize I'm completely fucking this up. This was supposed to be a private conversation during which I would calmly explain my rationale for not wanting the engagement while appealing to his probable desire for freedom. We weren't supposed to fight, and I certainly wasn't supposed to embarrass him in public.

I might as well have let Nikolai speak for me. The outcome couldn't have been worse.

Maybe there's still some way I can fix this. Dragging in a shaky breath, I reach over and clasp his big hand apologetically, ignoring the way my skin tingles from the warmth of his. "What I meant is... thank you. I love the ring, but can we please go and speak someplace private?"

The tiny muscles around his eyes tighten, but he gives a curt nod. "Let's go."

He leads me by the hand, ignoring the heads that turn to follow our progress. I can hear the titillated whispers in our wake, and a sick feeling invades my stomach. Announcement or not, we're now linked in these people's minds, our names to serve as fodder for the gossip mill for weeks or months to come.

Not only is this the first time anyone's ever seen me holding hands with a man, but he's a Leonov on top of it. The tongues will wag so hard they'll be in danger of falling off.

We exit the ballroom into the hallway leading to the restrooms, but Alexei turns in the opposite direction, lengthening his stride until I'm all but jogging to keep up. Stopping in front of one of the doors at the other end of the corridor, he pushes it open and pulls me inside before slamming it shut behind us. Only then does he release my hand.

I immediately back up a few steps. We're in another ballroom, a much smaller and empty one, where chairs are stacked legs up on top of a dozen round tables. Behind us is a stage with a large rolldown screen—probably used for lectures and presentations. I take all of this in on autopilot, having received training in situational awareness from Pavel over the years. He's also trained me in shooting and hand-to-hand combat—the latter being something I hope I won't need tonight despite the dark anger evident in Alexei's expression.

"Speak," he says grimly. "You have ten minutes before we need to be back for the announcement."

"Right, about that... I have some good news." I take a deep breath in an effort to rein in my runaway pulse. The only good thing about all the adrenaline flooding my system is that it's counteracting the fuzziness from the pills. I *am* making sense right now. I think. Regardless, I plow on. "My father is on board with postponing the announcement."

Alexei's eyes narrow. "What?"

"Yeah, isn't that great?" I lock my hands together in front of my ribcage to stop them from shaking. The ring presses into my skin, all cold metal and hard diamond. "He's leaving it up to us to decide the timing, which is the right thing, don't you think? That way, we can postpone the announcement for now and—"

"For now?"

"Or for a while." I swallow. "What's the rush, right? I'm sure you have better things to do at this stage of your life than deal with a fiancée who's been forced on you. Our parents, they're so medieval in their thinking, so—"

"We're not postponing a fucking thing." His jaw flexes dangerously. "If your father thinks he can welsh on the agreement—"

"No, no—no one's talking about that." At least not yet. I drag in another breath and drop my hands to my sides, consciously uncurling my fingers. I need to appear calm and rational, not scared and defensive. "Please, Alexei, listen to me. We have a choice now, you and I. *We* can decide what we want, not our parents."

His nostrils flare. "And what you want is to postpone the announcement?"

Fuck. This is going so much worse than I'd hoped. I'm not getting through to him. "We both want that. I'm sure you don't want to be engaged to me. You don't even know me."

He arches his eyebrows. "Don't I?" He advances on me, each step reminding me of a wolf's determined stalk. "I've been getting daily reports on you for the past three years. I know what you eat and how long you sleep, what you wear and which video games you play. I know all about your friends and your teachers… and your little cannabis hobby." Stopping in front of me, he smiles darkly at my stunned reaction. "Yes, it's true. You have no secrets from me, Alinyonok. I know about all of it—even the two pills you took an hour ago for your headache."

I should be freaking out over this heinous invasion of my privacy and its even more horrific implications, but my mind latches on to the most insignificant detail of all: the way he said my name. Most Russian names, mine included, have several informal variations, but nobody's ever called me Alinyonok. It sounds very close to *olenyonok*—baby fawn—and on anyone else's lips, it would make me feel all warm and fuzzy inside.

But not on his. Never on his.

He doesn't get to call me something so soft and tender—not when there isn't an ounce of tenderness in his murderous black soul.

I'm about to light into him with that when I realize the drug might still be scrambling my thoughts. There's no reason for me to care what he calls me. What matters is that he's been spying on me in the most invasive way possible, and the fact that he's been able to do it despite all of my family's security precautions —and more importantly, that he cares enough to do it —is beyond chilling.

"Why?" is the actual question that emerges from my mouth as I stare up at him. My heart taps out a sickening beat in my chest as I further process the implications. I have an awful feeling I already know the answer, but I press ahead anyway. "Why would you do that?"

He cups my face, the rough edge of his thumb

stroking over my cheek as his smile darkens further. "Why do you think, my beauty?"

Because he's not against the betrothal. He wants me. As he told me at the prom, he already regards me as his. I've been trying to convince myself that his behavior that night was nothing more than some territorial instinct run amok, that his possessive declarations didn't mean he actually wants me as his wife, but on some level, I've always known the truth.

"The betrothal…" I swallow as he lowers his hand to stroke my throat with his knuckles, his touch feather light yet devastating in its impact. "You want it."

"Are you surprised? I've wanted you from the moment I saw you." He trails his hand farther down, brushing his knuckles over my collarbone, then over the tops of my breasts, pushed up as they are by the corset-style bodice of my gown. Again, his touch is a mere graze, yet it feels as if he's painting trails of fire on my skin, reaching deep into my veins to ignite my blood. I swallow again as he adds dryly, "I know you're not oblivious to your looks."

My looks. Of course, what else? He doesn't want *me*. Nobody actually wants *me*. They want the pretty outer shell, the face and the body and the unique combination of genetics that's given the Molotovs this deceptively appealing façade. Eve's apples, my grandmother called us, an unbearable temptation that lures the innocent into a world of violence and sin. Not that Alexei is innocent in any way.

Like me, he was born into this dark world of ours.

Unlike me, he's embraced it fully.

The reminder is like a splash of icy water in my face. Stiffening my spine, I back out of his reach. "Well, *I* don't want this betrothal. Does that not matter to you?"

To my dismay, my voice shakes, the lingering heat of his touch unsettling me nearly as much as the burning hunger with which he watches my retreat. Equally disturbing is the knowledge that we're all alone in this room, that if he decides he wants me *now*, there's little I can do to stop him.

Sure enough, he comes after me. Instinctively, I back away, but he keeps coming until my back is against a wall and there's nowhere to run. But he's still not satisfied. He braces his hands on either side of me, caging me in as he leans closer. "Why not?" His voice is dangerously soft. "Why don't you want our betrothal?"

I stare up at him, struck dumb by the question. "Because I... because I don't." I've never thought about it in any sort of depth, but then again, why would I? One doesn't need a reason to not want a hurricane to strike—or to not be forced into a marriage with a man whose family is rumored to be even worse than mine. Boris Leonov is famous for his creative torture methods, and given what happened with Josh and my tutor, I know Alexei isn't all that different.

If I were to ever marry—and that's a big if—I'd want a husband who's the complete opposite of my father, not someone who's even darker and more brutal.

Alexei leans in even closer, until his face is mere

inches above mine and I can smell that subtle masculine cologne he wears, the one that makes me think of winter forests in the depths of night. "That's not an answer. What is it that you're objecting to? Me or the idea of marriage?"

"B-both." Dammit, why did I stutter? Fighting the urge to shrink back from his intense stare, I add in a steadier voice, "I don't want to marry, and I definitely don't want you."

"No?" Bending his elbow to lean on one forearm, he lifts his other hand off the wall to trail his fingertips over my jaw. A cruel curve appears on his lips as my breath catches in my throat, my body once again igniting from his touch. "You don't want me at all, Alinyonok? Not even a little bit?"

I don't trust my vocal cords to work, so I attempt a headshake. My heart is pounding so hard I'm certain he can hear it, and my skin is on fire where he's touched it and all around. Worse yet, I can feel an insidious slickness drenching my core, dampening the silky fabric of my panties. That empty, pulsing ache that plagues me so frequently these days is sharper than ever, making me want to squeeze my thighs together to relieve the worst of it. Except that wouldn't help, I know, and neither would pressing my hand against the spot where the ache originates. I need more, crave more—such as *his* hand there—but even with the pills clouding my mind, I know I can't give in to the urgings of my body.

Not if I want my freedom.

His smile turns crueler yet, even as savage hunger burns in his eyes. "Prove it then. Prove that you don't want me, and I'll let you walk away. Forever, if you want to."

Forever? As in… he'll let me out of the betrothal?

My heart throbs in my throat as I stare up at him, overwhelmed by a wild mixture of emotions. If it's true, if he means it… "Prove it how?"

His gaze drops to my lips. "A kiss." His voice roughens. "One proper kiss, that's all."

Oh, fuck. My head swims as a violent wave of heat washes over me and the ache between my legs intensifies. A kiss. It shouldn't be a big deal—probably wouldn't be for any other girl my age—but for me, it's Mount Everest.

It would be my very first kiss, something I've dreamed and fantasized about for years.

It would also play right into his hands because as inexperienced as I am, I know what my body's reactions signify. Physically, I want him. No matter how hard I've tried to fight it, his face is the one I always see in those fantasies of mine, his lips the ones I dream about when I envision my first kiss.

No.

I can't.

I won't.

At least that's what I plan to say, but he doesn't let me. Cupping my face in one big palm, he swoops in and takes what I haven't given.

My first kiss.

His lips are warm and soft against mine, his breath flavored with a hint of cinnamon. I gasp as he sweeps his tongue over the closed seam of my lips, and he ruthlessly takes advantage, invading the recesses of my mouth, overwhelming me with his taste, his scent, his feel… with sensations so intimate and novel that my eyes squeeze shut and my hazy brain shuts off entirely, leaving me at the mercy of my body and the scorching heat throbbing between my legs. I forget that I'm supposed to hate him, that he's the enemy who may soon deprive me of my freedom. I forget that this is a test I can't afford to fail and what will happen if I do.

I forget everything, and I kiss him back.

My arms wind around his neck, my body pressing against his in mindless need as I respond with all the hunger I've been suppressing, all the passion I've been denying. I can feel the hard bulge of his erection against my stomach, and it fuels the heated frenzy inside me, feeding the arousal that's been years in the making.

A low growl rumbles in Alexei's throat at my response, and his kiss turns violent, almost bruising. Because he's wanted me all this time too, I realize dazedly. Because his need is as strong as mine. Gripping my hair, he arches my head back, exposing my neck, and a choked moan escapes my throat as he drags his open mouth over it, his hot, biting kisses burning my tender skin. At the same time, he runs his other hand down the side of my body, his palm skating over my shoulder, my ribcage, the dip of my waist, the curve of my hip... His fingers close over the fleshy part of my ass, squeezing it hard, and then he bunches the skirt of my dress in his fist, pulling it up.

A distant alarm bell clangs in my mind as cool air washes over my bare legs, but it's quickly drowned out by a scorching new wave of sensations as his fingers delve between my thighs, locating the source of my throbbing ache under the soaked silk of my underwear.

"Fuck, yeah. You're so wet," he breathes in my ear, and hot shame washes over me, perversely heightening my arousal.

This is everything I've fantasized about and more, and the knowledge that he's the one touching my slick folds, that it's his fingers on my flesh, not mine, makes this both oh-so wrong and infinitely hotter.

I need to put a stop to this, right now, but I can't think with those clever fingers doing wicked things to me, can't voice a coherent protest with his teeth grazing over my neck, his tongue teasing the tender underside of my ear. All I can do is pant and moan, gripping the shoulders of his jacket, as the heated tension in my core builds and builds until it's like a coiled spring inside me. His fingers are now moving in a circle, somehow intuiting just the right rhythm, and my heart races madly as the sensations intensify unbearably. Every muscle in my body locks, my breath hissing through my clenched teeth as what feels like a tsunami rises inside me. Dark and potent, it carries me ever higher until I'm certain I'm going to die from it.

"That's it. Give in to it, my sweet beauty." His voice is

a soft growl in my ear as he pinches my throbbing clit, hard, and the tsunami wave crests and crashes down, wrenching me over the edge I've come close to but never crossed before. My mouth parts in a wordless cry as my inner muscles clench and release with cataclysmic, violent pulsations, and white-hot ecstasy blasts me apart. Only his hand between my legs and my death grip on the shoulders of his jacket keep me from sinking to the floor as my knees buckle, my muscles no longer able to hold me up as spasm after spasm racks my body.

Gently biting my earlobe, he releases his pinching grip on my clit, and I shudder as another, smaller shockwave causes my core to clench again.

Breathing raggedly, I open my eyes as he lifts his head, gazing down at me with savage satisfaction mixed with burning hunger.

"Your first?" he asks in a low, rough voice, and I nod on autopilot, my neurons still not firing properly. Distantly, I realize I'm shaking, my overheated skin cooling rapidly in the air-conditioned room as he withdraws his hand from between my legs and lifts it to his mouth. Pointedly, deliberately, he sucks each finger clean, the dirty action making me shudder with another, much weaker aftershock… along with shame and dawning horror.

What have I done? How could I have allowed him to do this to me?

I lick my swollen lips and taste the faint hint of cinnamon. Realizing I'm still clutching at his shoulders,

I let go and plaster my palms against the wall, needing to feel something solid in a world that's wobbling on its axis.

Alexei kissed me, and I didn't stop him.

He made me come, right here in this empty ballroom.

The enormity of it is too much to process. All I know is that I failed his test in the worst, most mortifying way possible. And he knows it too.

Victory shines in his coal-dark eyes as he runs the pad of his thumb over the edges of my lips and says gently, "You might want to fix your lipstick before we go back out there, Alinyonok. All eyes will be on us as we make the announcement. Later tonight, we can resume this."

He pushes off the wall and steps back, freeing me from the cage of his body, and a surge of panic chases away my mortification as the meaning of his words filters into my brain.

The engagement.

He plans to announce it right now… and then take me to bed.

My life as I know it ends tonight.

"Wait!" I call as he turns toward the door. I'm shaking even harder now, so overwhelmed by what has just occurred that it's all I can do not to break down crying. "Alexei, please, wait."

He turns back to face me, his eyebrows arched sardonically, and I know there's nothing I can say to convince him to stop, to make him believe that I don't want this. He gave me a chance, and I blew it.

I threw away my freedom for a kiss and an orgasm.

"Well?" He glances at his watch. "The music has already stopped, and the guests are gathering by the stage to hear a big announcement. We shouldn't make them wait too long."

"Alexei, please." Pushing off the wall, I stagger toward him on unsteady legs. My temples throb agonizingly as the headache I've suppressed returns with sudden violence, adding to the turmoil within me. My stomach churns with nausea as I say urgently, "Please, can't we just talk about it? I'm starting college in a few weeks. In New York City. I—"

"I know." His jaw flexes as I stop in front of him. "We do need to talk about that, but not right now. Either way—"

"Please." I grip his hand with both of mine, my desperation growing by the second. *Either way,* he said. Meaning that I might not be able to go to Columbia. Meaning that from this moment on, he expects to make all the decisions for me.

Like a horror movie reel, scenes from my parents' marriage flash through my mind, only instead of my mom's face, I see mine. And instead of my father, I see Alexei. I see him ruling my life with threats and blackmail, all the while manipulating my body and my emotions with the unholy attraction that he's already used against me tonight. I see an endless parade of parties and networking events where I'm expected to look beautiful and smile, even as everything that I am withers and dies inside. I see our children growing up with the bitter knowledge that their parents hate each other and passing on that hate to future generations, perpetuating the awful cycle.

I see it all, and a sob rips from my throat as the tears I've been trying to hold back spill over, streaking down my cheeks in hot rivulets. His face blurs in my vision, the hammers pounding harder at my skull, and I clap both hands over my mouth as my nausea abruptly intensifies. Only it doesn't help.

All I have time to do is lurch a few feet to the side before I fall onto my hands and knees and expunge the contents of my stomach onto the gleaming marble of the floor.

If I thought I was mortified before, it's nothing compared to the way I feel as strong hands clasp my shoulders, stabilizing me as more heaves rack my shaking body. "That's right. Get it all out," Alexei murmurs, smoothing back a few hairs that have escaped my updo to cling to my clammy forehead. "You'll feel better soon."

No, I won't. How could I, when he's seen me be utterly disgusting? Somewhere in the back of my mind, I'm aware that the likely culprit for this is the pills—either alone or in combination with the headache that's making me feel like my brain is imploding—but that doesn't help. I don't even have a napkin to wipe my mouth. Moaning in pain and embarrassment, I try to crawl away from the scene of my crime, but Alexei pulls me to my feet and lifts me against his chest.

Startled, I grip his shoulders as he carries me over to one of the tables, where he knocks one of the upturned chairs to the floor with his elbow and deftly flips it upright with his foot before depositing me onto it.

"Wait here, okay? I'll be right back," he says softly, squeezing my shoulder, and before I can reply, he strides out of the room.

Like an obedient dummy, I sit, too weak and shaky to move. A minute later, he reappears with several damp paper towels, a bottle of water, a travel-sized mouthwash, and an empty plastic cup—supplies that he no doubt pilfered from the nearby men's room. Crouching in front of me, he gently pats my lips with the damp towels, his manner as impartial as that of a nurse, and then he directs me to gargle with the mouthwash and spit into the cup. By the time I'm done with that, he's opened the water bottle and is holding it out to me. Gratefully, I chug it down, feeling more human with every swallow.

"Better?" he asks as I lower the empty bottle to my lap, and I nod, unable to meet his gaze.

He takes the bottle from me and sets it on the floor. "How is your headache?"

"Not so good," I mutter, wishing I had the power to just disappear from here. Like in the *Harry Potter* movies—poof and gone.

He tilts my chin up with curved fingers, forcing me

to look at him. His tone is gentle. "Do you want me to take you home?"

I blink, startled at the warm, almost sympathetic look in his dark eyes. "You mean..."

"We can go right now, get you into bed with an ice pack on your forehead. Then first thing tomorrow, I'll get you in to see a top neurologist, have them run some tests."

"Oh, no, thank you, I have an appointment with my parents' doctor this coming week and—wait, no." I press the heels of my palms to my throbbing temples. "I can't just leave. It's my party, and there are all these people—"

"So they'll party on without you. Who gives a fuck?"

I stare at him, my heart pounding erratically as I drop my hands. "What about the announcement? I thought—"

"Six months." His tone hardens, all traces of warmth fleeing his gaze as he rises to his feet. "I'll give you six more months to get used to the idea of us. Go to Columbia, study what you wish, and when you come home for winter break, we'll choose two dates—one for the announcement and one for the wedding itself."

For a moment, I'm certain I've misheard him about the six months. Stunned, I'm about to ask him to repeat what he said, but he's not done speaking yet.

"I'll give this to you on two conditions," he continues. "First, you will see a doctor for the headaches. Immediately. And second, no more pot or illegal drugs, prescription or otherwise." He bends over me, gripping the arms of the chair as his eyes drill into me. "Can you promise me that?"

"Yes! Absolutely." For six more months of freedom, I'd promise anything.

"Good. And there's one more thing…" His eyes are like black diamonds as he brings his face closer, his voice dripping with menace as he says softly, "Have all the fun you want with your friends in the Big Apple, but know this: any man who tries to touch you will regret it for the rest of his very short, very painful life."

Chapter 11

Present Day, Location Unknown

My cheeks burn as I stare into Alexei's eyes, unable to pull my hands away from where his palms are pinning mine to the table, the bright sunshine making it impossible to hide from the truth of his words.

I did want him as a young teen, even if I didn't understand it at the time. And by my eighteenth birthday, I was ripe for the taking. *His* taking. As much as I dreaded a forced marriage, I wouldn't have been able to resist falling into his bed after the party if the pills hadn't made me so sick.

Only I can't admit that now. I can't give him even more ammunition against me.

"I wasn't myself that night," I say unevenly. "I was high. You know that."

His jaw tightens, and he releases my hands to lean back in his chair. "Yes, you were. High and sick with it. And like a fool, I took pity on you, giving you those extra six months." His lips twist. "Little did I know what it would cost me."

Pity. So that was his motivation. I've wondered about that for years. Even after my world shattered that winter, a part of me remained curious about his motives that night, whether he'd given me the reprieve out of some semblance of kindness or because he'd found me repellent.

Now I know. And I don't know how I feel about it, whether it changes anything. Because another part of me, one that I only recently realized exists, has always resented him for those few extra months… that little bit of extra freedom that proved so costly for both of us.

If he'd pushed ahead with the engagement announcement on my eighteenth birthday, would I have been home that awful winter night, or would I have been in *his* home, his bed, far away from my parents' penthouse?

If I'd already been officially his, would the events of that night have even taken place?

My throat closes up, as it always does whenever I recall that terrible evening, and tension squeezes my temples in a merciless vise. Swallowing against a fresh wave of seasickness, I look down at the table, where my hands are now clenched together, my knuckles white… as white as the faint white scar on my right forearm. With effort, I unfurl my fingers, noting with a corner of my mind that my red nail polish is still intact, still unchipped. Unlike me.

I lift my gaze to Alexei's face, unshed tears burning like acid behind my eyelids. I shouldn't say it, I know, but the rebuke blasts from my lips, as illogical as it is revealing. "You should've stolen me then, right after that party."

"Yes," he says, and for the first time, his onyx gaze reflects pain. My pain. His voice is heavy with regret as he says, "I should have taken you then, no matter how sick you were. Or at the very least, I should've stopped you from returning home that winter evening, even though your six months weren't up."

Chapter 12

6 Years and 9 Months Earlier, Moscow

"Mama, I'm heading over to Natasha's," I say in a falsely cheerful tone as I stick my head into the media room, where my mom is glued to yet another soap opera. "I'll be home late."

She glances my way, her eyes red and swollen. Her voice is thick, clearly hoarse from crying as she says, "But you just flew in this morning."

"I know, but I made plans with Natasha weeks ago. She's really eager to see me." And I'm really eager to get out of here.

"Take a few bodyguards with you then." She returns her attention to the TV.

"I will, of course."

I can go now, but I hover in the doorway, uncertain of what to do. I'm dying to escape the toxic atmosphere in my parents' penthouse, but I've never seen Mama so upset, nor Papa so enraged and drunk. Rumor has it she's taken a lover, some government official who's so high up that even my powerful father can't take him out without consequences. I have no idea if it's true, but if it is, I hope that means my parents will finally go their separate ways.

It's long, long overdue.

She continues staring blankly at the screen as I chew on my lower lip, torn between my desire to leave and my need to comfort her. She wouldn't welcome the latter, I know—she likes to pretend none of us know about her discord with Papa—but I don't know if I can leave her like this. If at least Pavel and Lyudmila were here, they could look after her, but they both have the evening off.

Hesitantly, I step into the room. "Mama…"

"Just go," she says tonelessly, not taking her eyes off the screen. "I want to be alone."

I want to honor her wish, but some instinct propels me deeper into the room. Approaching her plush chair, I sink to my haunches in front of her. "Mama, are you sure you're okay?"

Her tear-glazed eyes meet mine, and her lipstick-covered mouth quivers in a forced smile. "Why wouldn't I be, Alinochka?"

As she speaks, her slim, perfectly manicured fingers play with her necklace, a heart-shaped diamond pendant on a thin gold chain that Papa gifted her upon Konstantin's birth. It's one of her favorite pieces of jewelry, and I often spot it on her neck after their fights. I suspect it's a way for her to remind herself of the good times, before she knew what the man she married was really like.

Carefully, I venture, "You seem a little upset. Is something going on?"

Her mouth quivers harder. "No, no. Just…" She reaches behind her neck and fumbles with the clasp of the chain. "Here." She grabs my hand and places the necklace onto my palm. "I want you to have it."

"Oh, um… thanks, but why?"

"I don't need it anymore." She attempts that shaky smile again. "I've worn it enough."

Or she's done trying to pretend that the good times —assuming there were any—are worth putting up with the hell that is her marriage now.

The rumors must be right. She and Papa are finally divorcing, and I can't say I feel anything but relief.

"Thank you, Mama," I say softly, closing my fist over the necklace as I rise to my feet. "I will treasure it."

"Oh, it's just a trinket," she says, waving her hand. "I'm sure Alexei will gift you much prettier things."

I freeze in the middle of putting on the necklace. "Alexei?"

She nods, looking a bit sheepish. "Did I forget to tell you? He's coming by to pick you up first thing tomorrow morning. Wants you to spend the day together. He didn't mention it to you? He was going to come by today, see you as soon as you got home, but his flight from Hong Kong was delayed."

"No," I say in a choked voice, dropping my hands. "He didn't mention anything to me."

The last time we had any interaction was at my eighteenth-birthday party, or rather, when he dropped me off at home with the admonition to rest and feel better. At least I think that's what he said. I was mostly out of it during the car ride due to the headache and the lingering effects of the pills. In fact, that whole evening is a blur. What I do remember clearly is that Alexei promised me six months, and six months from late July is not the end of December. I have almost four more weeks of freedom. Except… did he also say my winter break is when we'd decide the timing of everything?

Fuck. He did, and I totally blocked it out of my mind, latching on to the six months as if it were a date carved in stone.

Idiot. I don't know what I was thinking. No, it's more like I *wasn't* thinking. I was so giddy at the unexpected reprieve that I threw myself into college life with the reckless abandon of someone who has six months left to live. I took all the classes, went to all the parties, did every extracurricular activity I could, and whatever free time remained in my jam-packed schedule I spent exploring every nook and cranny of New York City, from well-known museums to invitation-only poetry slams in basements on the Lower East Side.

For the majority of the past five months, I was busy from the moment I opened my eyes at sunrise until I passed out from sheer exhaustion after midnight, and the only time thoughts of Alexei were able to invade my mind was at night, in my nightmares and dreams. Even on the plane ride over here, I was frantically fixing a bug in the app I wrote for my Intro to Computing class, so I could send it to my professor and score some extra credit.

To Mama, I must look like a deer in headlights because she says with fake brightness, "Well, now you've been informed. Have fun at Natasha's, okay? Say hello to her family for me."

"I will, thanks." On autopilot, I walk out of the media room and head to the front door, all the anxiety I've been holding at bay with nonstop activity hitting me at once.

Alexei.

He wants to spend a whole day with me.

Tomorrow.

What the fuck am I going to do?

My head begins to ache. Hoping that the freezing evening air will stave off a full-blown migraine attack, I pull on my warmest boots, hat, gloves, and coat, and send a text to the bodyguards waiting downstairs that I want to walk to Natasha's and thus don't need a car.

I'm already halfway to the elevator when Papa's hulking frame appears in the doorway. "Going out?"

His words are slurred, his face bloated and unshaven. His black hair, now liberally sprinkled with gray, is a disheveled mess, as are his clothes, with his white shirt stained and buttoned askew, the tails half-tucked into his partially unzipped slacks. No tie, no shoes of any kind, only one sock on his left foot.

I've never seen my powerful, handsome father look like this, not even when he was drunk out of his mind in the past.

"You okay, Papa?" I ask softly, an unfamiliar pity stirring inside me.

The man in front of me has never been the kind of dad they show in movies, the one who hugs you, has important talks with you, and generally acts like you're more than an object to trade away. Still, he's my father and he's hurting. However broken and toxic his relationship with Mama has become, at one point he loved her, I'm sure. Maybe he still does, in his own twisted way.

He snorts and stabs his fingers through his hair, the gesture uncharacteristically erratic. "Why the fuck wouldn't I be?" He lurches toward me, his movements reminding me of an overcaffeinated zombie. "So you're going or what?"

I take a wary half-step back and lift my hand to hide the pendant hanging around my neck. "Yes, to Natasha's. I'll be back in a couple of hours. Is that okay?"

He jerks his chin toward the door. "Yeah. Get the fuck out of here."

Rude, but okay. I don't need to be asked twice. I hurry into the elevator, and when I come out into the lobby downstairs, four bodyguards join me. Once we emerge onto the street, they fall back to follow me discreetly, and I'm left alone with my thoughts—thoughts that immediately turn to Alexei.

Delayed in Hong Kong, Mama said. Did he go there for business or pleasure? I spent a few days there last summer, visiting a friend from school, so I can picture the glamorous nightclubs and lounges, along with all the gorgeous women. Women that I can all too easily imagine in Alexei's bed, their lithe bodies writhing against him, their full lips wrapped around his—

Fuck. Stop. I don't care. He can fuck all the Hong Kong beauties he wants—whatever keeps him away from me. There's no reason for me to feel like throwing up at the thought of him touching some other woman. I should be glad if his attention is elsewhere. I should hope it's elsewhere.

Maybe, just maybe, at this very moment, he's with a woman who'll make him forget all about our stupid betrothal, and then I'll be free for good.

The thought should cheer me up, but I feel even worse, my headache intensifying by the minute. Even the crisp winter air doesn't help. It's cold out tonight, at least minus twenty degrees Celsius, and ice crystals crunch under my boots as a frigid gust of wind hits me in the face, making me shiver and wish I'd taken the car after all. Or maybe even stayed home, toxic atmosphere and all. I could've ignored my parents, taken my headache pills, crawled into bed, and caught up on some much-needed sleep.

Well, too late now. I keep walking, trying not to think about seeing Alexei first thing tomorrow, and as I'm rounding a corner, a black car pulls up to the curb next to me.

Startled, I jump back, my instincts screaming of danger, but my bodyguards are already there, forming a semi-circle between me and the car. Their hands go to their weapons as the darkened window in the back rolls down, revealing a familiar pair of dark eyes set in a hard-featured face.

Eyes that gleam with cruel amusement.

"Easy, boys," Alexei drawls as I stare at him, frozen in shock. "I mean my intended no harm."

Pushing open the door, he steps out, unfolding his tall frame in a smooth, easy motion as I gape at him, unable to utter a word.

How is it possible that he's here, standing in front of me, when he's supposed to be in Hong Kong?

My stunned gaze travels over his face, with its hard angles and sharp planes, then over his body, the powerful muscles of which are visible even in the gray leather jacket he's wearing over a black sweater. Dark jeans hug his long, athletic legs, and black biker boots cover his feet, making him look even more dangerous.

"Miss me, Alinyonok?" he asks, coming toward me, and my bodyguards fall back, melting out of sight once more. They must've been notified about our relationship, such as it is.

I almost call them back, but I don't want Alexei to know just how much he scares me. Instead, I stiffen my spine and paste on a cool smile. "What are you doing here? I thought your flight was delayed."

"The storm petered out, and my pilot decided to risk it," he says, stopping in front of me. The streetlights reflect in his eyes, making them look like black mirrors above me. His lips curve mockingly. "I knew you were anxious to see me."

I fight the urge to flinch as he lifts a hand to tuck a strand of hair into my hat. Unlike me, he's not wearing any gloves, yet his fingers are warm despite the freezing cold outside. So warm that they burn my chilled skin and make me feel like I'm wearing too many layers of clothing… like I need to be naked in this frigid weather to cool the fire raging inside me, and even then, I might burn up alive.

"Anxious, yes. To see you, no," I force myself to say as he pulls back his hand. My heart is racing, but I can't let him know that. I need to project a cool, calm demeanor, so he doesn't realize how much he's unsettled me. How unprepared I am to face him and everything my future holds.

The taunting smile remains on his lips. "You wound me, my beauty. Here I am, risking my life by flying in a snowstorm to see you, and you couldn't even wait for me at home."

I clench my jaw. "I have plans with Natasha tonight." Which he, stalker that he is, probably knows about.

His smile broadens. "You'll have to cancel those, I'm afraid. Since I've made it home in time, you and I have plans tonight. Big plans."

My heart rate intensifies. He can't possibly mean… "I have four more weeks!" To my embarrassment, the words come out in a squeak. With effort, I get a hold of myself and say in a more level tone, "I don't have to see you until late January." At which point, I'll be back in New York City, and he'll hopefully be too busy to fly in to see me.

The smile falls off his lips, and his eyes tighten dangerously. "What the fuck are you talking about?"

"You…" I swallow, my heart hammering faster at his expression. "You gave me six months."

"I gave you until this winter break."

"That's not six months!"

A muscle ticks violently in his jaw. "I didn't mean that literally. I told you we'd talk when you came home, decide all the dates then."

He did tell me that, but all I heard was six months. And I need that extra month. I need it badly. Raising my chin, I say evenly, "Your poor math is not my problem."

His nostrils flare as a harsh gust of wind blows ice crystals off a roof and into our faces. "Oh, but it is." He grips my elbow. "Let's go. We'll discuss this in the car."

"No!" I dig my heels in as he pulls me toward his car. Instantly, my bodyguards surround us, their presence lending me courage. They won't let me get taken against my will, not even by my so-called intended. I raise my voice so they can hear me clearly. "I'm not going anywhere with you."

He stops, fury burning in his eyes as one of the bodyguards—Vankov—moves aside his jacket, revealing a gun holster, and says, "Please let go of Alina Vladimirovna." Even in a tense situation, he doesn't forget to show respect by using my patronymic. Jaw set firmly, he continues. "She has no wish to go with you."

Yes. Go, Vankov!

Except Alexei doesn't obey. Nor does he look the least bit intimidated. "She's my fiancée," he says in a hard voice, "and we have things to discuss. Step aside, or you'll regret this."

The other guards exchange concerned glances, but Vankov pulls the gun from the holster and aims it at Alexei. "My orders are to protect the Molotov family. Release her and step back, sir."

Alexei's eyes narrow into slits, but he releases my elbow. Thank God. For a moment, I was afraid he might try to take me anyway, four armed guards notwithstanding.

Just in case, I back away, and his eyes track me with the intensity of a cat watching a mouse slip out of its grasp.

"One more night," he says grimly as two guards step between us, shielding me with their huge bodies. His gaze pins me through the gap between their shoulders, the heat in it making me burn despite the icy wind. "I did tell you six months by mistake, so I'll give you one more night to get used to the idea of us. But no more. I'm done waiting, Alinyonok. First thing tomorrow, I'm coming for you, and nothing and no one will stop me."

I'm still shaking with cold and adrenaline as the elevator doors open and I walk into my parents' penthouse. I didn't go to Natasha's after that confrontation. I couldn't. Instead, I turned around and ran home, needing the safety of its walls, illusory though it might be.

One more night. That's all I have now. Tomorrow, he'll come, and my parents won't lift a finger to stop him. Unlike my bodyguards, they won't care if he drags me away. In fact, Papa will likely assist him.

Raised voices reach my hearing as I take off my coat and hang it in the closet by the door before pulling off my shoes, hat, and gloves. It takes a while because my fingers are so numb from the cold I can't feel them. The voices grow in volume as I walk toward the staircase, my head throbbing agonizingly. I need my pills, a hot shower, and my bed, in that order. What I don't need is my parents fighting yet again.

God, I hope they separate soon.

"—fucking whore," my father is shouting in the living room as I creep toward the staircase, desperate to hide in my room before they realize I'm home. "I'll fucking kill him!"

"You try and see what happens! I'm leaving, and you can't fucking stop me!" My mom's voice is high-pitched, hysterical. A crash follows—some priceless mantel piece going flying, no doubt. I wince and cover my ears, but even that doesn't block Mama's voice as she shrieks, "And I'm taking Alina with me! Fuck your alliances. She hates him, just like I hate you!"

I stop halfway up the stairs and drop my hands to listen. Does she mean it, or is this just something she's saying to wound my father? And if she does mean it, would she be able to actually keep me out of Alexei's clutches? Maybe if my brothers were to side with her—

Another crash makes me jump. "She's my fucking daughter! You try to take her, and I'll fucking kill you. I'll fucking kill you both, along with that motherfucker you're fucking!"

Another crash is followed by Mama's pained cry. My heart jackrabbits into my throat. I've never heard my father say that to her, nor have I ever witnessed him physically hurting her, though I've suspected it's happened.

Shaking, I pull out my phone from my pocket and dial Nikolai's number. He's the only one in Moscow right now. Konstantin is in Dubai on business, and Valery is doing his army thing somewhere near Crimea.

The phone rings as another crash sounds, followed by a louder cry of pain.

Please answer, please answer. Come on, please answer.

"Yeah?" Nikolai's voice drawls in my ear, and I nearly collapse in relief.

My middle brother will come here. He'll know what to do.

"Kolya, they're fighting again," I say, all but tripping over the words. "It's bad. Like really bad. I think he's hurting her."

"Fuck!" He doesn't sound as surprised as I would've

liked. “Stay away from them. Don’t intervene. I’ll be right there.”

The line goes dead, and I stick my phone back into my pocket with trembling fingers as I head toward the living room. I want to do what Nikolai said and hide out in my room until he arrives, but I can’t. Not when Mama is getting hurt.

Another crash, another feminine cry of pain, more violent cursing. I break into a run, my heartbeat roaring in my ears. “Papa, Mama,” I shout as I round the corner to the living room. “Stop, both of you!”

But I’m the one who stops dead, paralyzed in horror at the scene in front of me. My father is straddling my mom on the floor, and she’s no longer crying out in pain. She’s silent, unconscious, as he slams his massive fist into her face, over and over again.

A face already so bloodied and pulverized it’s barely recognizable as hers.

Stop. Stop. Stop.

I can feel my lips forming the word, but no sound leaves my throat as my gaze frantically bounces around the room, seeking something, anything—there! A knife, right there on the floor, next to my parents.

I don’t question its presence. I just act. Leaping forward, I snatch it in my right hand and grab my father’s elbow with my left, just as his fist is about to slam into Mama’s face again. “Stop!” This time, the word emerges in a shriek. “Papa, stop it! Please, stop!”

He knocks me off my feet with one swipe of his

powerful arm and hits her again. I leap up, heedless of pain, and try to stop him again. He slams his fist into my solar plexus, sending me flying, and resumes his pummeling of Mama's face. My back slams into the arm of the couch and my vision darkens as I wheeze for air, but I bounce up and come at him again, knife gripped tightly in my fist.

I don't want to hurt Papa, but I have to stop him. I have to get him off Mama, no matter what it takes.

He's so consumed with rage he doesn't notice as I grab his arm again and slash down with the knife, aiming at his shoulder. It's not what Pavel taught me, but this is Papa, not some random stranger in an alley. I want to bring him back to his senses, not kill him.

The knife sinks shallowly into the thick muscle of his shoulder, and it's only when he turns on me with a roar and I see his eyes that I realize my mistake.

His pupils are blown so wide they cover most of his irises.

He's not just drunk. He's on something way stronger.

In an eyeblink, he's on me, violently grabbing my arm with the knife. Something cracks in my wrist as he wrenches the knife from my grasp, but the cry of pain dies in my throat as he slams his fist into my ribs, making me stumble back, doubled-over and wheezing. It takes a couple of seconds for my vision to clear, and when it does, I charge forward with a scream. "Don't! Stop!"

He doesn't.

Straddling Mama's unconscious body, he slashes at her chest with the knife, again and again. Blood sprays everywhere, all over the white furniture and the gleaming wood floors.

Screaming, I slam into him at a full run and succeed in knocking him off her. We roll on the floor, and I somehow end up on top. I jump off him and leap to my feet, but he's only a second behind me. With a roar, he comes after me, knife slashing wildly, and I feel fire lick down my forearm as I frantically use it to shield my face.

He's going to kill me, I realize distantly as he raises the knife again, and then a massive force slams into my stomach and everything goes black.

A coppery smell, mixed with something foul, fills my nostrils as I wake up to the sound of men grunting and furniture breaking. My vision is foggy as I open my eyes, and I have to blink several times to bring the images into focus. My forearm burns, my ribs and stomach feel like one giant bruise, and my head throbs nauseatingly, but none of that matters once I realize what I'm looking at.

Nikolai and our father, locked in a deadly fight.

Blood covers them both as they roll on the floor, wrestling for control of the knife.

Adrenaline floods my veins, propelling me to my feet. My head swims, my vision darkening again, but I ignore it and lurch forward. "Stop," I croak, stumbling toward them. "Please, stop."

I trip over something and fall onto my hands and knees. White-hot pain shoots up from my right wrist, and I rise onto my knees, instinctively cradling it against my chest. There's blood on me, I notice dazedly, so much blood. It's dripping from my arm and covering the floor as far as the eye can see. I didn't realize I had that much blood in me, that anyone had that much blood in them, not even—wait, I was going somewhere.

I jerk my head up and see that Nikolai is now on top of Papa, pinning him down. He also has the knife.

Finally. It's over.

Except… Nikolai's face is a mask of dark fury, his hand gripping the knife in a lethal hold I recognize from my lessons with Pavel.

Bile climbs up my esophagus.

No, please, no.

"Kolya, stop, please." The words are but a hoarse whisper. I try again, my desperation growing. "Kolya, please!" I begin crawling toward him on my knees and the one hand that's intact. "Stop. Stop now."

He doesn't listen.

As Papa reaches up to grab the knife, my brother evades his grasping hand and slices down, the deadly motion lightning quick.

Blood. More blood. It sprays everywhere, all over Nikolai, all over me. A scream rises in my throat and bursts out, and now, now Nikolai looks my way, his blood-splattered face pale and no longer twisted with rage.

Only it's too late.

Lying pinned underneath him is the unmoving corpse of our father, his guts spilling out through the torso-length opening inflicted by his son's lethal blade.

Another scream builds in my throat, but it doesn't come out. It dies inside me because my eyes land on the other body in the room.

Mama.

At least I think it's Mama.

It could also be a person-shaped, bloody piece of meat covered in shreds of clothing.

No. Please, no.

I crawl toward it, ignoring the pain stabbing up my arm, and when I get there, I realize it is her. Or rather, what used to be her.

What's left can't even be considered human. Papa sliced her up beyond all recognition.

A keening wail comes from somewhere, a cry of agony so gut-wrenching I can't bear to hear it. I clap my palms over my ears, but the wail keeps going until thickly muscled arms wrap around me, pulling me against a blood-drenched shirt.

"Shh, Alinochka. Quiet down. It's okay. It's going to be all right." Nikolai's rasping voice might as well be that of a stranger. Same goes for his blood-covered face when I twist out of his hold and scoot backward. I don't recognize this man kneeling in front of me… this violent killer who can't possibly be my brother.

Shaking, I push up to my feet. I feel cold, so very, very cold. Numbly, my gaze travels from Nikolai to the bloodied lump that used to be our mother and then to the gutted corpse that used to be our father.

My knees buckle, and this time, when the darkness comes, I welcome it.

I never want to see the light of day again.

Chapter 13

Present Day, Location Unknown

Breaking eye contact with Alexei, I push up from the table in a sharp motion and stride over to the side of the boat, where I grip the wooden rail and stare out at the endless blue ocean, my chest heaving with uneven breaths. The memories press down on me, so heavy they suffocate me even after all these years.

My father killed my mother.

My brother killed my father.

I saw it all, and not a day has passed since that night during which I haven't thought about it, haven't remembered… whether consciously or in my nightmares.

Warm hands land on my shoulders from behind, strong thumbs digging into the tightly knotted muscles around my neck. It helps. The painful tension eases, the worst of the memories receding even as my spine goes rigid for a different reason… one that has nothing to do with that night.

"I'm sorry about what happened with your parents," Alexei says softly, continuing the insidiously soothing massage. "I wish I'd known right away, but your brothers did a good job of covering it up."

Yes, they did. As far as our family's friends and acquaintances were concerned, my father died of a heart attack, and my mother perished in a car accident on the way to the hospital. And even these fake facts were kept out of the papers by the sheer force of my family's influence, to cut down on unsavory speculation.

"How did you find out the truth then?" I ask, trying to ignore the effect his touch is having on me. "Was it through my therapist, as I suspected?"

"Yes." There's no remorse in his tone, no guilt at this terrible invasion of privacy. "I had to know what was happening with you, so I could decide what to do."

I squint against the sunlight reflecting off the water. "And what did you decide?"

He steps closer, pressing his body against my back and hooking his hands on the rail on either side of me, once more caging me in his embrace. Resting his chin on top of my head, he murmurs, "I decided to give you more time. Time and space to heal."

Yeah, sure. Because he's such a saint. "You were just afraid I'd slit my wrists if you came near me."

He's silent for a beat before admitting quietly, "That too."

Chapter 14

6 Years and 9 Months Earlier, Moscow

"How do you feel?" Lyudmila asks softly, perching on the edge of my bed. "Can I get you anything?"

"Painkillers," I mumble, squeezing my eyes shut against the stabbing agony behind my eyelids. "More painkillers, please."

Everything hurts. My fractured wrist, my slashed forearm that required twenty stitches, my bruised ribs and stomach, and most of all, my head. It's the aftermath of a concussion, the doctors told me. I must've hit my head during the car accident, the one that injured me and killed my mom last week.

They don't know anything, of course. There was no car accident. My injuries are from the fight with my father, the concussion from when he threw me against the wall and I blacked out. Also, these injuries aren't the reason I didn't attend my parents' funeral three days ago, like the public thinks.

"Here, take these." Lyudmila helps me sit up and swallow two pills with a glass of water. The movement makes my ribs scream in protest, and I fall back onto my pillow with a groan, fighting a wave of nausea.

A cool, wet towel is laid gently over my forehead, relieving the worst of the stabbing pressure, and I take small, shallow breaths until the nausea passes and my thoughts begin to run together. A warm haze envelops me. These pills are the good stuff, not the weak bullshit I've been taking for the headaches since Alexei gave me that six-month reprieve. Nor are they the useless crap the doctors prescribed me in the first few days after the "accident" because of the stupid concussion. It took me writhing in agony for three days straight to get them to relent and give me actual painkillers. But now I have them, and they're my best and only defense against the pain that threatens to consume my every waking moment.

The hours compress into minutes as I drift, pleasantly high and numb. When my mind starts to clear, I have Lyudmila give me two more pills, and once she leaves the room, I take two more on my own.

I don't want to think, don't want to process what happened.

I just want my mind to stay blank.

At some point, my brothers visit me. Konstantin, his face pale and drawn with grief. Valery, as cool and unreadable as always. Nikolai, who looks terrible, his chiseled jaw covered with a week's worth of stubble and his eyes ringed by dark shadows. His visit unsettles me so badly I can't stop crying for two hours, and then my head hurts so much I send Lyudmila out for a doctor.

The doctor comes, makes sure my healing is on track, and prescribes a stronger painkiller. He warns me not to take it until later today, when the other pills will be out of my system, but I don't listen. As soon as he's gone, I down the new pills, and when they make me throw up, I wait a few minutes and take them again—and manage to keep them down. They take effect almost immediately. My world turns hazy, all soft and nebulous, and the pain recedes until it's but a distant memory. Same goes for the urge to cry. I can't even recall why I was crying.

I fall asleep some time later, only to wake up from a nightmare with a scream that brings Pavel and Konstantin—who has temporarily moved into the penthouse to keep an eye on me—running into my bedroom. Once they confirm there's no real danger, they question me about my physical and mental state before exchanging worried looks and leaving. A minute later, Lyudmila comes in and makes me eat something, then gives me another dose of the pills, which I supplement with a dose of my own a few minutes later.

Anything to keep lucidity at bay.

Hours stretch into days as I drift in and out of drug-induced semi-consciousness. I'd prefer to be knocked out completely, but sleep is when the nightmares come, so sleeping pills are a no-go. Hazily, I wonder if I'm breaking my promise to Alexei by taking all this medication. For five months, I kept my end of the bargain. After my disastrous eighteenth birthday, I didn't smoke a single joint, nor take any drugs that weren't prescribed to me. Then again, what I'm taking now *is* prescribed to me.

These pills are legally mine, and I need them.

I need them because the alternative is facing reality, and I can't bear to do that.

Alexei came by again, Lyudmila told me this morning. Or maybe it was sometime yesterday—I can no longer tell what day it is. Either way, my brothers refused to let him in. He's apparently been demanding to see me since the morning after everything went down, but they've managed to keep him away.

My head throbs at the thought of it all—at the thought of *him*—even though there's no longer any reason to be afraid. My father's death has rendered the betrothal contract null and void; Konstantin told me that a few days ago. Nikolai heads up the family business now, and he has no interest in being allied with the Leonovs. There's no reason for me to see Alexei ever again, and I'm glad. I think if the engagement were still on the table, I'd take that entire bottle of pills and be done with it.

Now, more than ever, I can't imagine marrying a man like my father. Not even if some tiny, pathetic part of me wishes I could feel Alexei's arms around me one more time, to experience the heat that burns between us instead of the icy numbness that engulfs me when I think about that night… about anything, really.

It's best that I don't think at all.

I reach for the pills and swallow two more without bothering with water.

THE PILLS RUN OUT EVENTUALLY. OF COURSE THEY DO. And my brothers, sadists that they are, refuse to get me more until I agree to go to therapy. Apparently, now that several weeks have passed, my injuries have healed enough for me not to require constant pain medication —or at least that's what the doctor told them. Fucking bastard. What does he know?

Either way, I have no choice.

For the first time in weeks, I dress, put on makeup, and make my way downstairs, where the car awaits. I feel weak and nauseated, my legs shaking and my head pounding with each step I take. By the time I get into the car with the usual posse of bodyguards, I'm sweating and my stomach is cramping with anxiety.

I manage to compose myself a bit during the ride, but I'm still a mess when I enter the office of Yekaterina Belkova, the therapist. She turns out to be a thin, petite woman with warm brown eyes and an inviting smile. To my embarrassment, half an hour into our session, I break down crying, even though we've only spoken about the early years of my childhood, back when my parents' marriage was just marginally terrible.

She waits considerately until I've pulled myself

together, and then we talk some more. Instead of the usual hour, my brothers have booked me unlimited time with her today, and as we go on, I find myself glad about that. I haven't spoken to any of my friends since that night. I can't, not when they have no clue what truly happened. Nor can I really open up to my brothers. We're not that close, emotionally speaking, and I'm certain they're suffering from trauma also, in their own way. The last thing I want is to add to their burden.

That's why it's such a relief to talk to this sympathetic, nonjudgmental woman, even though I'd still rather have the pills. She doesn't push, doesn't probe, just asks thoughtful questions and listens. We meander from topic to topic, and somehow, I end up telling her about Alexei and the betrothal that has given me so much anxiety over the past three and a half years —yet another thing I've never told my friends about, nor discussed in any depth with my family.

My brothers knew I was against the betrothal, but they never understood how much Alexei terrified me and why. But Belkova understands. Right away, she comprehends how dreadful it would've been for me to end up like my mother, trapped in a love-hate relationship with a ruthless, violent man.

"You must be so glad the betrothal is over," she says softly, and I nod, wrapping my arms around my stomach as it cramps painfully again.

She regards me with those warm brown eyes. "Have you spoken to him since your parents' deaths?"

Deaths. My chest tightens agonizingly, and acid tears sting my eyes again. "Deaths" is such a bland way of putting it, so simple and generic.

Fuck, I wish I had the pills.

"I'm sorry," she says, immediately intuiting the source of my distress. "Do you feel up to talking about that? About… the accident?"

I clench my hands together until my knuckles turn white. My stomach churns violently, and cold sweat pops all over my body, even at the roots of my hair. I don't know if I'm ready to talk about it—or if I'm even allowed. Then again, she said that last word carefully, with a pause. She's not taking the official story at face value, either because of something I've let slip today or because my brothers have given her some kind of heads-up.

I swallow thickly and force the words past the tightness in my throat. "Is everything I say in here completely private? Even if it's not entirely… legal?"

She regards me unblinkingly. "Yes. Not only do I have to abide by doctor-patient confidentiality as part of my professional oath, but I have a special agreement with your family. Nothing you tell me, no matter how disturbing, will leave this office." Gently, she adds, "Not even if it's about murder."

Murder. That's the right word. Or more precisely, uxoricide and patricide.

The memories bubble up, dark and toxic, and I turn away to take short, shallow breaths as bile rises in my throat. Maybe I'm not ready to talk about it, no matter how much I want to. Maybe all it will do is cement the images in my mind, etch them in deeper until that night is all I can think about and no amount of pills can help.

"We don't have to talk about that today if you're not ready," Belkova says quietly. "It's entirely up to you."

Yes, yes, it is. I control this. The knowledge calms me. Maybe I *should* talk about it. That's why I'm here, after all. Maybe sharing what I have witnessed will free me from the crushing weight of that burden, from the grief that chokes me and poisons every breath I take.

Maybe the doctor will work some magic, and I will stop thinking about how nice it would be to take the entire bottle of pills and never feel this way again.

Digging my nails into my palms, I turn back to face her. She's waiting patiently, not saying anything, and slowly, haltingly, I begin to speak. I tell her about my encounter with Alexei and how it drove me to return home early. How I heard my parents fighting and called my brother. How I went to intervene, not waiting for him to arrive, and what happened after. As I go on, the words come faster until they're pouring out of me in a torrent, a vile sludge that now feels as uncontrollable as the tears pouring down my face. As unavoidable as the one truth I couldn't bear to face until this moment.

The knowledge that my parents' last argument was about me.

"That doesn't make it your fault," Belkova says, leaning forward. Her face is pale—I guess my tale is too much even for her. Resolutely, she continues. "You have to know that. Anything could've set off your father in that state."

But it wasn't anything. It was Mama's threat to take me with her. It was her telling Papa that I hated Alexei. And that's not all. Violently, I shake my head. "I should've gone to them right away. As soon as I heard them fighting, I should've intervened instead of calling Nikolai. I—"

"Then you'd be dead as well." Her voice strengthens with conviction. "This is *not* your fault. You are not to blame for this in any way. Your father—"

"Enough!" I shoot up to my feet, shaking. Why did I think this would make me feel better? Talking to this stranger who can't possibly understand? There's no magic assurance she can offer, nothing she can say that will bring the bloody lump that was my mother back to life or make my brother any less of our father's murderer. Worse yet, she's wrong. It's one hundred percent my fault. There are so many things I could've done differently, so many ways I could've prevented this. If I'd stayed home that evening, if I'd said just the right thing to Papa before leaving, if I hadn't been away at school in the prior months… The "ifs" are endless, infinite, each one burrowing into my mind, tearing away pieces of my soul. For weeks, I've been blessedly numb, my thoughts hazy, but with every minute that passes without the drugs, they become clearer and sharper until they slice as agonizingly as Papa's knife.

Belkova is speaking again, saying some more

soothing bullshit, but her words don't reach me. Spinning around, I run out the door and into the elevator. I don't stop running until I'm in the car, and even then, my heart won't stop racing, my hands trembling as I stare out the window, unseeing, flashes of that night hitting me one after another, blasting me with all the emotions the pills have been holding at bay.

I'm only vaguely aware of the honking behind us and the black SUV pulling up alongside our car. It's not until we swerve sharply and the bodyguards curse, drawing their weapons, that I realize something is happening.

From the front passenger seat, Vankov is shouting at the driver, "Don't let that motherfucker force you off the—fuck!" The black car rams into us from the right, and the brakes screech as we veer left. If not for my seatbelt and for the bodyguard sitting next to me, I'd have been thrown across the car. As is, I grab on to the seat in front of me with a strength born of a sudden surge of adrenaline.

Attack.

We're under attack.

A part of me can't believe it. I mean, I have security for a reason, but still. It's broad daylight, and we're a few minutes' drive from the center of Moscow. One would have to be suicidal to attack the Molotov family so openly.

The driver slams on the brakes so suddenly my head whips forward and the seatbelt cuts into my ribcage, squeezing all the air from my lungs. We screech to a halt. Fuck! We nearly crashed into a van that's appeared out of nowhere to block the road ahead of us. The driver attempts to reverse, but something rams into us from behind, forcing the car to stop again.

Boxed in. We're boxed in, I realize as the bodyguards swear again. In addition to the van in the front, there are three SUVs—one on each side of us and one behind us. They've forced us off the main road onto this side street, ignoring any and all witnesses. My pulse revs up higher. I can only think of one enemy of ours who would dare be so bold, so brazenly—

And there he is.

The van door facing us slides open, and out comes none other than my former intended, Alexei Leonov himself.

Dressed in all black like the angel of death, he comes toward me with long, furious strides. His expression matches his clothes, his eyes glowing darkly and his jaw tightly clenched.

For a moment, I'm so struck by the sight of him—and by the heat that flashes under my skin—that I can't move a muscle. Then panic whips through me as five more men jump out of the van after him and eight more emerge from the SUVs on either side of us, armed with semi-automatic rifles.

There's no way my four bodyguards could fight them and win.

"Holster your guns," I say shakily, fumbling with my seatbelt as my bodyguards jump out of the car to confront the danger. "It's okay. I know him."

And I know he won't hesitate to kill anyone who stands in his way.

Vankov grits his teeth but does as I ordered. The other guards follow his example.

Meanwhile, Alexei reaches my door and yanks it open. His eyes burn into me. "Get out. Now."

I open the door on the opposite side and scramble out of the car, my heart pounding wildly. For the first time in weeks, I feel alive. Alive and terrified. I can only begin to guess at what Alexei wants, and none of the guesses are reassuring.

At my small defiance, his eyes narrow and he rounds the car with the same furious strides, reaching me before I can even think about running. Gripping my elbow, he drags me to the van and pushes me into one of the rows of seats in the back, then climbs in and slides the door shut behind us, isolating us from the men outside.

As soon as he lets go of my elbow, I scramble across the seat, as far away from him as I can get in the close confines of the van's cabin. My breath comes fast and shallow as his eyes lock on me, still narrowed, still furious.

And then, just like that, I'm furious too. "What the fuck do you think you're doing?" I stop shrinking against the window and jut out my chin, glaring at him. "My brothers—"

"Fuck your brothers." His jaw works violently as he braces one hand on the seat in front of us, trapping me in place. "I've been trying to see you for weeks."

"So you came with a fucking army to run my car off the road?"

"Would you rather I used said army to storm your residence? That was on the agenda for this Sunday, but luckily, you emerged from your lair before that."

I suck in a shocked breath. He was going to try to force his way into the penthouse despite all the guards and security measures? "Why?" is all I can find the wherewithal to ask as I stare into his grim face.

His mouth twists. "Why do you think?" Dropping his hand, he takes in a visible breath. Some of the fury leaves his gaze, his tone softening minutely as he says, "I wanted to talk to you, express my condolences for your loss… make sure you're healing okay."

My loss. Right. For a second, I'd almost forgotten. I swallow thickly, my anger receding, and his expression softens further.

Leaning forward, he lays his hand on my leg, his touch impacting me even through the thick layer of my coat. "Alinyonok…" His eyes hold mine captive. "I'm sorry about the accident. I really am."

Accident. Even he doesn't know. I jerk my leg away, my anger reigniting. "So sorry you were going to force your way into my penthouse? Is that why you ran me off the road with your fucking fleet of cars? To express your condolences?" My voice rises with every word. "Why can't you just leave me the fuck alone? It's over. We're done. Finished. This stupid contract is—"

"In force until I say otherwise," he says, his expression hardening. Whatever warmth I imagined in his voice is gone, his face set in cruel, harsh lines once more. "I don't give a fuck what Nikolai says. You were promised to me and—"

"I'm not a fucking object!" I shriek, all my emotions suddenly coming to an explosive boil. I shake from the force of them, my stomach churning violently. I can feel myself unraveling, falling apart strand by strand, piece by bloody piece. Like Mama. Like the bloody piece of meat that was all that remained of her at the end. Like Papa's guts that spilled out under Nikolai's ruthless blade. The blade that I can once again see flashing toward my face, cutting a fiery line down my arm... *Stop! Stop! Stop!* The word blares like an alarm in my ears, and I realize I'm screaming it out loud, my fists hammering against the only available object—Alexei's chest. Somehow, I'm on him, fighting him, shrieking something incoherent. Distantly, I hear him curse, and then he wraps his arms around me, restraining me. It doesn't help. His embrace only maddens me. I lose all control, screaming and sobbing and biting like a wild animal until I finally collapse against him, my skull imploding with agonizing pain.

I don't know if I pass out or if my brain simply shuts down for a while, like a computer needing a reboot, but the next thing I'm aware of is being carried up the stairs and toward my bedroom. Angry male voices surround me, and I dimly recognize that it's my brothers arguing with Alexei. That's who's carrying me, I realize with a vague sense of shock—Alexei. Gently, he deposits me onto my bed, where I curl up into a ball, clutching my head and moaning. It feels like a chainsaw is cutting through my skull, slicing apart my brain.

"Shh, it's okay. Here." A female voice now. Lyudmila. She shoves two pills into my hand, and I have just enough strength left to bring them to my mouth and dry-swallow. A glass of water with a straw is placed next to my face, and I suck up a few sips before squeezing my eyes shut against the awful pain.

"You see this?" Nikolai's voice is hard and biting. It reaches me through the pounding agony in my head. "That's *your* doing. She was already on the mend, getting off the meds, and now this shit again. You need to stay the fuck away from her, you understand?"

Alexei's tone matches his. "What the fuck is wrong with her? Has she seen a doctor?" he demands, and I force my eyes open long enough to see him glaring at Nikolai, the two of them standing nose to nose. Konstantin is next to them, his posture tense, ready to intervene in case things go south—as is Pavel, who's looming in the doorway like a human mountain.

"That's none of your fucking business, but yes," Nikolai says through gritted teeth. "Now get the fuck out before I rid her of you for good."

Alexei's posture shifts ever so slightly, but I've been around dangerous men enough to comprehend the lethal tension in his stance... to see the menace in the way Alexei's muscles coil, like a cobra preparing to strike. My pulse spikes, anxiety twisting my stomach.

"Stop," I whisper, pushing up onto my elbow. Then

stronger, "Stop!"

All the men freeze and turn to look at me.

Alexei is the first to move. He comes toward me, his long strides bringing him to me in three steps. His face is tense, worried. "Alinyonok…" He sits on the edge of my bed and reaches for me. Instinctively, I shrink back, and he stops, his expression altering as he drops his hand from midair. Something almost like pain flashes in his dark eyes, and then Konstantin and Nikolai are there, grabbing his arms to drag him off the bed.

"Don't!" I cry out as Alexei twists out of their hold with a swift, savage movement. The sound of my own voice sends a shard of agony through my eyeballs, and I fall back onto the pillow with a groan, pressing the heels of my palms against my throbbing temples.

All three of them go still again. Then Alexei starts toward me, and my brothers step in his path, grim determination on their faces. They won't let him near me, I realize—and he won't leave without a fight.

Violence is all but inevitable, and I can't bear the thought of it, the possibility of any of them getting hurt.

"Let…" Battling the pain in my skull, I push up to a sitting position and swallow against a rising tide of nausea. "Let him talk to me alone. Please."

Nikolai flashes a sharp look in my direction as Konstantin asks, frowning, "Are you sure?"

"Yes. Please. You can—" I swallow convulsively. "You can be right outside the door."

Nikolai and Konstantin exchange glances, then

reluctantly step aside. They don't leave the room, however. They stop by the door and watch stonily as Alexei approaches me again. Stopping at the head of my bed, he opens his mouth to speak, but I forestall him.

"I don't want you," I say, staring up into his midnight eyes. My voice is soft but firm, each word crisply enunciated despite the cloud beginning to engulf my mind, dulling the pain and blurring the unbearably sharp edges of reality. "I don't want our engagement. I don't want to date you. I don't want any of it. If you care about me at all, you will walk out of here now and leave me be. I'm not yours. I will never be yours willingly. I would sooner die."

His face tightens more with every word I speak, his jaw clenching until the tiny muscles by his ears pulse violently. He says nothing as I fall silent. He just looks at me, and I hold his gaze without blinking, ignoring the hammers pounding at my brain and the veil of the drug blessedly creeping over my mind. In this moment, I mean every word I say, and he knows that. I can see it in his eyes, in the way they darken further, in how his features harden until there isn't a trace of emotion left on his face. Not even anger.

Without uttering a single word, he turns and leaves—and I fall back against my pillow, drained. It's not until my brothers step out of the room as well, following him out, that I break down and cry, overcome by a sorrow that makes no sense... by a sense of loss I can neither comprehend nor name.

Chapter 15

Present Day, Location Unknown

"That day in the van, you didn't know what happened that night. You thought it was an accident. So when did you find out the truth? Did you hack into Belkova's records or simply bribe her?" I ask hoarsely, turning around in the cage of Alexei's arms.

He releases the railing and steps back, giving me a little breathing room. I know it's just an illusion, though.

No matter what he has said, he's never truly given me space. Not in all the years that he's ostensibly stayed away.

"I broke into her office that night and read her notes," he says, as if that's normal. As if that's what every man who wants a woman does. He tilts his head, regarding me with an inscrutable expression. "How did you realize that I knew?"

"My brothers. I overheard them talking about a run-in with you a few days later," I say. "You must've said something to them because Konstantin was wondering how you might've found out. His vote was for the hacker theory."

Alexei's gaze turns speculative. "Is that why you've never gone back to Belkova?"

"Belkova or any other shrink." Just the possibility that he might've gotten a glimpse inside my head was enough to prevent me from talking to one ever again, no matter how much my brothers urged me to give therapy another chance.

"I'm sorry about that." He sounds genuinely regretful. "That's not what I intended."

I scoff. "What did you intend?"

"To understand what happened. To—" He stops and shakes his head. "It doesn't matter now."

"Doesn't it?" A gust of cool, salty wind whips my hair into my face and makes the boat pitch underneath us. I grip the railing with one hand and push the hair off my face with the other. A storm is forming on the horizon; I can see the ragged edges of the gray clouds in the distance, blocking out the bright blue of the sky. It's still far from us for now, but it's coming. I can feel it. Just as I can feel the danger in the man in front of me. Staring up into his face, I ask, "Why did you bring me home that day?"

He arches his eyebrows. "What would you have had me do? You were hysterical in my van, then near-catatonic. It was either bring you home or take you to a hospital—and believe me, I strongly considered the second option."

I laugh humorlessly. "Why not a kidnapping? I mean, you had me in your clutches."

"Is that what you wish I'd done?"

"I wish you'd left me alone, like I'd begged you to."

One corner of his mouth curves up. "Do you?"

"Yes!" I drag in a calming breath and modulate my tone. "Of course I do. I told you, I don't want you in my life. I never did."

"What life?" He takes a half-step forward and leans in, forcing me to press my back against the railing. His eyes glint harshly. "You didn't have a life. At best, you had an existence."

"Thanks to you!" Forgetting all caution, I glare up at him. "You ensured I'd be alone, went to great lengths to make it happen."

"And yet you didn't get your brothers involved." He cocks his head. "Why? Is it because deep down, you wanted my attention? Because you knew you'd miss it if it were gone?"

My mouth drops open. "What? No! That's insane. I never wanted—that's bullshit."

"Is it?" He brushes another windswept chunk of hair off my face, his touch making my body feel overheated despite the cooler air brought by the rapidly advancing storm. I instinctively draw back, and his lips curve mockingly at my reaction. Gripping the railing on both sides of me again, he leans in and says softly, "You had no idea what you wanted, my beauty. You still don't. But I will show you. And once I do, you'll realize how wrong you were to send me away all those years ago. You'll understand the truth of us as well as I do."

Chapter 16

3 Years and 4 Months Earlier, New York City

"You're coming to my premiere tonight, right?" Risha asks, drumming her taupe nails on the table. At my lack of response, she leans in, brown eyes narrowed. "Right?"

"Of course. I'll be there." I take a sip of my mimosa and steal another glance out the window. Yep. The man is still there, loitering across the street. I'm pretty sure he's not part of my security detail, so he's got to be *his*. Fuck.

"Hey." Risha snaps her fingers in front of my face. "Earth to Alina."

I blink and refocus on my friend. "Sorry, what?"

"I asked if you're bringing anyone, so I know how many seats to reserve for you, and you totally ignored me. Again. What's going on with you?"

I force a smile onto my lips. "Nothing. Just thinking about finals."

"You'll ace them, I'm sure," Risha says and waves at

the waiter. As we wait for him to make his way across the crowded restaurant, she says, "So? Are you bringing anyone or not?"

"Not."

"Oh, come on. Seriously?"

"Fine. I'll ask Natasha. She's flying in from Moscow this afternoon. If she's not too jet-lagged, maybe—"

"That's not what I meant." Risha gives me an exasperated look. "I'm talking about a guy. Or a girl who's not a platonic friend. Or—fuck, I don't know—a bear. Whoever, whatever you're into."

I grin. "I'm not into bears, I promise."

She regards me dubiously. "If you say so. How about my friend Lana then? She—"

"I'm not into girls either."

She pounces. "So guys then? How about Julio? He—"

"No." My voice comes out harsher than I intended. I take a breath. "No Julio, no Raj, no Dennis, no Lana, no setting me up with anyone. I've told you that a million times."

"But—"

"But nothing. I don't need any help on the dating front."

"Yeah, right," Risha mutters, but at that moment, the waiter comes, saving me from her badgering. We place our brunch orders—buckwheat crepes for me, an egg-white omelet for her—and once he's gone, I pepper Risha with questions about her upcoming movie and she forgets all about my lack of boyfriends.

As she speaks, I steal another glance out the window. The man is gone, but I don't feel relieved. He's just out of sight, I know. He and whoever else Alexei hired to stalk me.

A familiar tightness squeezes my temples at the thought, and I take deep breaths, trying to focus on Risha's chatter in an effort to stave off the headache. I've been better this year, going entire weeks without taking so much as an Advil, and I intend to keep it up. This is the first spring in years during which I've felt more or less like my old self, and I'm not going to let Alexei's goons set me back.

I didn't go back to school after that awful winter break. I stayed in Moscow, battling debilitating migraines and a depression so deep I wasn't sure I'd ever emerge from it. But I did come out of it after a few months, thanks to a cocktail of antidepressants and specialty painkillers that reduced the duration and frequency of the migraine attacks. And thanks to the fact that Alexei left me alone—or so I thought at the time. It wasn't until I returned to college the next fall and attempted to resume normal life that I learned the truth.

If he can't have me, neither can anyone else.

I didn't date at first. I had my hands full trying to catch up on all the classes I'd missed, and the recurring headaches didn't help. I ended up switching my major from Computer Science to Economics and Political Science because staring at a screen while writing code for hours on end made the headaches worse. Plus,

Econ and PoliSci were easy for me, and I needed easy. Though my depression had lifted enough for me to function, I still had more bad days than good.

By the end of the summer semester, though, I'd caught up and was back on track to graduate with my classmates. And at the start of my junior year, I was finally ready to date, despite a frequent sensation of being watched that I ascribed to lingering anxiety and paranoia.

The first guy who kissed me fell off a rooftop bar the next evening. A drunk accident, everyone said, but it shook me so badly I didn't go on another date until many months later, when I met Jorge in a nightclub during my spring break in Bali. He was clever, funny, and had eyes so dark they looked almost black. I liked him immediately. We danced, made out a little, and agreed to meet on the beach the next morning.

He never showed up. The following day, I learned that he'd died the morning of our intended meetup. Apparently, he was riding to the beach on his scooter when his brakes failed and he went over a cliff.

A terrible accident, everyone said again, but I knew better this time. It was no accident that men kept disappearing and dying around me.

It was *him*.

Alexei wasn't done with me.

That realization triggered my worst migraine attack in a year, one that took me several weeks and two bottles of pills to recover from. I missed the end of the spring semester and had to take summer classes to make up for it. I also began paying extra attention to my surroundings, no longer writing off my feelings of being watched as paranoia. I started evaluating everyone around me as a potential stalker, and now, every once in a while, I'll spot them—one or more men following me who aren't part of my regular security detail.

I've considered talking to my brothers about it, telling them about the threat still posed by Alexei, but the relations between our families have grown increasingly tense, with several instances of business sabotage that were just short of open war, and I don't want that tension to escalate all the way to bloodshed because of me. I have too many deaths on my conscience as is. Besides, I don't think Alexei actually wants me anymore. We've crossed paths at various Moscow events in recent years, and he's ignored me as if we were strangers.

This stalking is his way of punishing me for breaking our betrothal, nothing more. I'm almost sure of that.

So here I am, just a few weeks away from my college graduation and still a virgin with zero prospects of losing that virginity. It would be sad if I actually cared, but weirdly, I don't. In a way, it's taken some pressure off of me. After I returned to school, I felt the need to prove to myself and to others that I could be like everyone else, that I was fully recovered. Catching up on classes was my number one priority, but resuming a normal social life was a close second.

I didn't want a boyfriend so much as I simply wanted to move on, to forget the past with all its ugliness. I didn't even care that I felt next to nothing when I kissed those two guys; I just wanted to have that experience.

Turns out, I can't—and that's fine with me. Something died in me the night my parents were killed, I've realized. Or maybe it was never alive in the first place. My sexuality had only begun to awaken when I was betrothed to Alexei, and from that moment on, it's always been tangled up with him—and with dread, fear, and shame. To this day, all my sex dreams, all my dark, dirty fantasies, feature him. Despite the horrible things he's done, I still want him, and I hate myself for that.

It wouldn't be fair to date another guy, even if that wouldn't place him in mortal danger. It wouldn't be fair to sleep with him while picturing my stalker in his place.

"Seriously, are you even listening?" Risha snaps her fingers again, and I give her a sheepish smile.

"Sorry about that. You were saying…?"

She blows out an exasperated breath. "Forget it. Are you high today or something?"

"Or something," I mutter, glancing out the window again.

Maybe I *should* get high to rid myself of this anxious feeling.

Come to think of it, that doesn't sound like a bad plan at all.

A blinding flash goes off as I approach the restroom, and I blink against it, annoyed. The paparazzi have no business photographing me. It's Risha and the other stars of her award-winning independent film they should be interested in. I lengthen my stride, mentally thanking my dress's designer for including the thigh-high slit in the tight, floor-length skirt, and before long, I've escaped the young reporter and her camera. Once I'm safely inside the luxurious bathroom, I lock myself in a stall, pull out the joint I just bummed off Giles, and take a few puffs.

There. Much better. I can already feel the tension in my temples easing.

I smoke the rest of the joint and flush the butt down the toilet. Then I wash my hands, touch up my makeup, and return to the party before Risha can accuse me of disappearing on her.

The screening is about to begin, so I head into the theater. Everybody is already seated, but two places in the center of the middle row are empty. One of them must be mine. Sure enough, it has a discreet label with my name on it attached to the back. The label on the other empty seat states, "Lion Holdings." Probably one of the companies involved in the production.

The theater lights dim, a spotlight falls onto the stage, and the movie's director emerges. He gives a speech, thanking everyone for attending the premiere and being involved in the movie. I only half-listen to his words, the pot making me feel pleasantly hazy. The actors are next, starting with Risha, who has the main role. I clap enthusiastically for her, and then I zone out again as the other actors give their speeches, thanking the director, the executive producer, all the other producers, the special effects crew, the costume design team, and so on.

Finally, it's time for the movie itself. The theater goes completely dark for a moment, and as the massive screen on the stage lights up with the opening credits, a tall, broad-shouldered man enters my row and takes the empty seat next to me. I glance at him, more out of courtesy than any real curiosity—only to stiffen in shock and disbelief.

Sitting next to me, staring at me impassively, is none other than Alexei Leonov, my former intended and current stalker.

The monster who I thought—hoped—no longer wanted me.

Chapter 17

Present Day, Location Unknown

"Lunch is ready," Larson's voice announces from behind Alexei, and I breathe a sigh of relief as my captor steps back, freeing me once more.

The floor pitches underneath us as we head to the table, which is now set with all manner of delicacies. The wind is blowing hard in my face and the waves are intensifying, the sky rapidly darkening. I almost stumble as the yacht tips sharply, but Alexei steadies me by gripping my shoulders, his hands strong and warm. Keeping his hold on me, he leads me to the table, where he pulls out a chair for me before taking a seat himself. As he drapes a cloth napkin over his lap, he glances up at the sky and says, "We'd better eat fast. It looks like the storm is going to reach us soon."

Larson nods, uncorking a bottle of champagne. "It'll pass quickly but could get rough for a bit. Might be best to head inside after you're done here."

Great. Rough seas. Just what I need. On the plus side, despite the growing waves, my seasickness is abating. Whatever drug Alexei used to knock me out must be clearing out of my system—that or I'm finding my sea legs.

Larson moves to pour the champagne into the crystal flute in front of me, but I stop him by covering the glass with my hand. "None for me, thanks." I meet Alexei's gaze across the table. "I have nothing to celebrate."

Alexei doesn't reply, but the corners of his mouth pinch in. Sensing the rising tension, Larson quickly fills Alexei's glass, places the bottle into a bucket of ice on the far edge of the table, and tactfully disappears.

I take a calming breath and reach for the plate of caviar sandwiches, one of the many traditional Russian dishes on the table. Antagonizing Alexei probably isn't the best idea, but I can't help it. Each minute we spend together winds me tighter, reminding me of things I've been trying to forget… like the way he shadowed my life for years upon years before finally making his move.

The way he controlled me, mind and body, long before I was his actual captive.

Chapter 18

3 Years and 4 Months Earlier, New York City

For a few heartbeats, I simply stare at him, at the hard features of his face illuminated by the flickering light of the screen. The movie has started, the haunting music from the opening scene enveloping me with its unnerving beauty. Finally, I force my lips to move. "What are you doing here?"

My words are barely audible, but he understands. His eyes gleam in the darkness as a mocking curve appears on his lips. "Attending the premiere of the film, same as you. My company provided the majority of the funding, after all."

Lion Holdings. Leonov. Of course.

I open my mouth, only to close it. Maybe it's the pot muddling my thoughts, but I can't think of a single response that wouldn't sound moronic. The obvious question is why he'd fund my friend's movie, but I already know the answer.

It's part of his revenge scheme, this elaborate,

ongoing punishment he's devised for me. It wasn't enough for him to have his henchmen stalk me from a distance and off any man who tried to get close to me. Oh, no. That was too merciful, so he's invaded my life in this new, even more disturbing way.

He doesn't wait for my reply. Turning away, he settles back in his seat and fixes his gaze on the screen, as if he's actually here for the movie and not to drive me mad.

I'm so stunned I keep staring at him, taking in his strong profile and the way his dark hair has gotten longer in the front, how his tux hugs his powerful shoulders and the way he takes up the entirety of his seat and then some, commanding every inch of the space around him. Belatedly, I become cognizant of the way my heart thuds loudly against my ribcage and how my lungs fight for air with stiff, shallow breaths, so I tear my gaze away and fix it unseeingly on the screen as I try to think past the shock and make sense of what's happening.

Alexei Leonov has funded Risha's movie, and now he's here, sitting next to me. Does that mean he's decided he wants me again? Or has he never stopped wanting me and has just been biding his time?

What does it mean that he's stayed away for three-plus years, and now he's less than a foot away from me?

I want to get up and run, to escape to the safety of my apartment, but there's no way I'd be able to explain my sudden departure to Risha. Or to Giles, who's flown all the way from California to attend our friend's big US premiere. Or to Natasha, who's currently sleeping off her jet lag in my bed and will ask all sorts of probing questions if I return home three hours early.

Besides, I don't want to give Alexei the satisfaction of knowing how deeply he's unsettled me. Let him think I'm as unbothered by his presence as he seems to be by mine. After all, I'm a Molotov, and we've survived everything from Mongol invasions to the Communist regime. What's a two-hour movie next to your enemy in comparison?

Pulling in a deep breath, I attempt to focus on the drama unfolding on the screen, but it's futile. The air I inhale brings with it a faint whiff of his cologne, and though we're too far apart for me to feel the warmth of his body, I'm aware of him on that primitive, purely animal level, his proximity making my nerves vibrate like guitar strings. Worse yet, I can feel the treacherous heat gathering under my skin, speeding my heart rate and soaking my silk thong. That carnal, sexual part of me that I've been all too happy to ignore in recent years has reawakened, and no matter how hard I try to focus on the movie, all I can think about is him. His hands. His body.

The way he made me feel on my eighteenth birthday, back when I was still mostly whole.

A shudder ripples over my skin as the memories threaten to invade my mind, and I focus my gaze on Alexei again, choosing the lesser evil. He turns his head in that moment as well, and our eyes meet, the flickering light from the big screen alternately highlighting and hiding the stark lines of his face, the dangerous gleam in his black-diamond eyes. My breath shallows out again, my lungs battling to pull in enough oxygen, and I feel dizzy from the heat burning inside me… from the intensity of the need that makes my core pulse with an empty ache.

His gaze drops to my throat, then trails down to my collarbones and the exposed swells of my breasts, pushed up by the tight bodice of the dress. My mouth goes dry, and I swallow hard. The built-in bra is too thick to betray the erect state of my nipples, but I'm breathing fast and he can see that. He can tell how agitated I am, how helplessly turned on.

I want to look away, to pretend I don't feel the magnetic pull between us, but it's impossible. As his eyes return to mine, I can no more turn away than sprout wings and fly. All I can do is sit there, quivering, as he slowly, deliberately, reaches over and lays his left hand on my right thigh, exactly where my skirt is slit, exposing a sliver of bare skin.

His touch jolts me. The feel of his hand on my naked thigh is like an electric shock, scorching every nerve ending with a violence that steals my breath and makes my heart feel like it's exploding. Only the presence of other people around us keeps a startled gasp from escaping my lips. Some distant part of me is still cognizant of where we are and how wrong this is.

And it is wrong. So, so wrong. He's my enemy, my stalker… a murderer of innocent men. I should dread his touch, be repulsed by it, yet I don't move away as he wedges his callused thumb deeper under the soft velvet of my dress, forcing the slit to widen as he holds my gaze, his eyes full of dark hunger and wicked knowledge. I don't jump up as he slowly, tauntingly edges his hand higher up my thigh underneath the dress. I don't flee as his fingers brush the edge of my thong, then delve underneath the damp silk to where my bare flesh is hot and slick, pulsing with need.

I just sit there like a statue, frozen and burning, trembling with shame and arousal, as the music in the film swells and crests, the audience around us whooping and clapping at whatever is happening on the screen.

I'm high. I must still be high to let this happen. Except I know I'm not. I have a high tolerance for weed these days, and the joint I smoked is no longer clouding my mind. But I tell myself that it is, that the drug is the reason I'm sitting here, letting him touch me so intimately in a theater full of people, where anyone can look over at us at any time and see his hand on my leg, inside my skirt.

No, it has to be the pot. It's making me do this, allow this.

His eyes burn into mine as he separates my wet folds and brushes his fingers over my aching clit. Just a light stroke, that's all it is, yet my entire body goes taut, my lungs seizing from the power of the sensation. He rubs the same spot again, his mouth curving wickedly, and I shudder from the sharp, biting pleasure as the agonizingly sweet tension coils ever tighter in my body, building to a sensory crescendo, taking me to the edge of that dark, mind-bending ecstasy I've only ever known at his hands.

The same big, strong hands that are touching me now with a skill and delicacy that can't—shouldn't—coexist with all the cruelty they're capable of… all the blood they've spilled.

The grim thought sobers me just enough to grab his wrist. It's strong and solid, the bones thick underneath the crisp cuff of his shirt, and I'm so caught up in the sensation of *me* touching *him* that it takes me a moment to realize he's not stopping, that my gesture, weak as it is, is being completely ignored. Instead, the hunger in his eyes grows darker, more predatory, his face taking on a demonic visage as he moves his fingers over my clit in a firmer, more purposeful motion, utterly disregarding my attempt to pry his hand away from me. At least I think that's what I'm attempting by tugging on his wrist. I may also be urging his hand to move faster, harder, to hurtle me over that tantalizing edge until my mind dissolves and I forget everything, including how much I should hate this.

And I hate it. I swear I do… right up until the very second when I shatter. My eyes squeeze shut, my teeth grind against each other to hold in a cry, and streaks of purple and white blast my vision as my inner muscles squeeze and release in a series of spasms that send dark ecstasy surging through my body, curling my toes inside my stilettoes and raising gooseflesh on my bare arms.

The orgasm is so strong it feels like it goes on forever. It's not until the sensations recede that I find the strength to open my eyes and face him… my nemesis who's just made me come.

He's still staring at me, his hunger unabated, his fingers on my swollen, throbbing, overly sensitive flesh. Blood rushes to my face, and I suck in a breath, mortified to realize what I've just done… what I've let happen and where.

My paralysis vanishes, and I let go of his wrist to leap to my feet. Turning left, I push my way past the spectators in my row, heedless of their grumbling, all my thoughts centered on escape. I'll apologize to Risha later, tell her I got another headache. She'll forgive me; she always does. Besides, it's not a lie. The intense mortification is swiftly giving rise to the familiar vise-like tension, all the blood that flooded my face transforming into hammers pounding at the inside of my skull. The stabbing needles will follow soon, blurring my vision and making me want to die, and the only hope I have of stopping this is to reach my pills in time.

My pills. My apartment. My bed.

I focus on that as I run out onto the street and flag down the nearest cab, not waiting for my bodyguards to bring over the car. There's no time for that, not when he might be coming after me, demanding that we continue, that I give him what he's now given me twice.

That I give him everything, my mind and body, my hopes and dreams, my very soul. The way my mother gave all of herself to my father, only to find that it wasn't enough... that a monster can't sheathe his fangs, not even for the one he loves.

My cab is already pulling away from the curb when Alexei emerges from the building, the look on his face matching the stark black lines of the tuxedo suit hugging his powerful body. He scans the street, his dark brows furrowed, and I yell at the driver to go faster, to step on the gas before it's too late.

It's not until we're several blocks away that I realize I'm crying, the tears rolling down my face and ruining my carefully applied makeup. And it's not until I'm at my apartment, shooing Natasha out of my bed as I frantically swallow a handful of pills, that I wonder what the fuck I'm going to do now that Alexei knows I still want him.

Now that I've shown him just how much power he holds over me.

Chapter 19

Present Day, Location Unknown

Dropping my gaze to my plate, I take a bite of my caviar sandwich and chew slowly, trying to focus on the rich, salty flavor of the salmon roe and the smooth, cool fattiness of the butter spread over the crisp French baguette. I try to focus on anything but the tense silence that stretches between us and the memories that intrude into it, memories that make my face burn and my heart race.

Like Risha's premiere. Like what happened nine months ago.

Unable to help myself, I look up from my plate and meet Alexei's gaze. He smiles darkly, and somehow, I know we're on the same page… that his mind is traveling along the same pathway, reliving the same events.

"After Risha's premiere," I say, both to break the silence and because I genuinely want to know, "I was afraid you were going to force yourself further into my life. Or do something like this." I gesture vaguely to indicate my current situation. "Yet you didn't. You left me alone again. Why?"

He picks up his champagne glass and takes a sip. "Because you weren't ready." His tone is even, matter-of-fact, as if everyone knows a woman must meet certain criteria to be violently abducted. As if all of this is perfectly logical, rational.

"Ready for what?" I ask, matching his tone. "To be forced into your bed?"

"We both know force won't be required."

I flush hotter but maintain the coolness of my voice. "Whatever you need to tell yourself to sleep at night."

"I don't plan to do much sleeping tonight."

Damn him. The flush spreads down to my neck and chest, and my breasts suddenly feel constricted, overly confined by the bra I'm wearing. The lacy fabric rubs against my peaked nipples, irritating them, and my thong feels uncomfortably damp. Unable to bear his dark, mocking stare, I return my gaze to my plate and focus on devouring the caviar sandwich, even though food is the last thing I want.

"You asked your professors for an extension on your final papers and exams," he says, his tone turning grim. Startled, I look up at him as he continues. "It was the worst migraine attack you'd had in years, so bad you didn't come out of your apartment for a week after the premiere. You barely got your schoolwork done in time for your graduation."

I nod slowly. I should be surprised or outraged that

he knows, but I'm too used to his stalking. "So that's why you stayed away for the next two years?"

He regards me over the rim of his glass. "It triggered you, our little encounter that night. Undid a lot of the progress you'd made. That's how I knew you weren't ready."

"How considerate of you."

My words drip with bitterness, but he just takes a sip of his champagne and sets down the glass, his expression unchanged. "I knew there would come a day when things would be different," he says as the yacht pitches sideways from a particularly strong wave. Casually steadying the glass before it tips over, he continues. "I knew you would recover, and once you did, I'd be there, waiting. Not that it was easy to be patient."

"Oh, really? You want a cookie? Should I pat you on the head for your restraint?"

A wicked smile stretches his lips. "You can pat me anywhere you want, Alinyonok. All of my heads are quite eager for your touch."

The flush assaults my face again, and my inner muscles clench on a sweet, sharp ache. Damn him. Damn him. Damn him. It's his fault I'm so fucking inexperienced that his innuendos make me blush. His fault I've never even truly flirted with a guy, instead putting up a cool, untouchable façade at all the parties and social events. *Ice Princess*, they've started calling me in recent years, and I wish I could be that. I wish I could turn off the sexual part of me, the part only *he* has ever been able to ignite.

"Fuck you," is the bright response I manage, and he lets out a low, rough laugh.

"Soon," he promises, reaching for a caviar sandwich of his own. "Right after this meal, in fact. It's time we finished what we started last winter… long past time, don't you think?"

Chapter 20

9 Months Earlier, Moscow

I hate December in Russia. I used to love it, with all the New Year's decorations on the streets and the festive atmosphere in all the shops and restaurants, but ever since the winter my parents died, I've despised this month. Normally, I go away somewhere, like Greece or Turkey or the Cayman Islands, but for some reason, Nikolai demanded that our entire family gather today at his loft, forcing me to cut my Switzerland ski trip short.

I especially don't want to be in Moscow because I know *he* will be here.

Alexei.

I haven't seen him in person since Risha's New York premiere, but I know he tracks my every move. His men are always there in the background, watching, waiting. For what, I don't know, but I've grown so used to their silent, hidden presence that it's as if they were own bodyguards. What amazes me is that my bodyguards don't seem to be aware of them. Well, for the most part. A couple of times, Vankov did raise an alarm after spotting someone following me, but he's never been able to catch anyone.

Alexei's men are good.

After my last encounter with him, I was so sure he was going to push for more that I decided to finally talk to my brothers and seek their help. I kept procrastinating on it, though, and as weeks stretched into months, I realized that my fears were groundless. Alexei isn't done playing this strange, remote cat-and-mouse game with me. He hasn't left me alone—if anything, I've been spotting more of his men around me—but he has stayed away, letting me go about my life without interference.

It's helped that I've done my best to avoid being where he is. After getting blindsided by his appearance in New York, I've been discreetly keeping tabs on his movements. While my brothers inherited the bulk of our parents' wealth, I have plenty of my own money, and I used a portion of it to hire a PI firm that my brothers know nothing about. The firm's job is to keep me informed about all things Alexei Leonov, which is how I know that for the past year and a half, he's been traveling all over Central Asia and the Middle East, building out the Leonov empire. And this is also how I know that last week, he returned from Tajikistan to attend the funeral of his younger sister, Ksenia, who was killed in a car crash, leaving behind a young son.

It's an awful tragedy for the Leonov family, and as

much as I despise Alexei, I can't help but sympathize with the pain he must be feeling. I can't imagine losing any of my brothers. All week long, I've been battling a bizarre urge to reach out to him and… do something. Express my condolences, maybe? Say I'm sorry for his loss?

No, that can't be right. I know better than anyone how pointless such platitudes are, how more often than not, they add salt to a raw, gaping wound. So I don't know what it is that I want to do, but the urge is like an itch under my skin, invading my thoughts at random moments during the day and keeping me awake at night. The last thing I need is to be in the same city with Alexei, lest I give in to this urge in a moment of weakness.

Fortunately, I'm not in danger of doing anything stupid tonight because I have to hurry to Nikolai's place. Whatever he wants must be serious because while my middle brother has taken on the role of the de facto head of the family, he's never mandated a family meeting before.

Everybody is already gathered in the living room by the time I walk into Nikolai's luxurious, modern loft. I like it more than the penthouse I've inherited from our parents, but I'd never tell Nikolai that. For the past few years, he's been pressuring me to move in with him or one of my other brothers, but I refuse to live my life under their watchful eyes. It's bad enough that Pavel and Lyudmila, who still reside with me, report to my brothers on everything I feel and do. Living with Nikolai would be an especially bad idea, as we haven't gotten along since that night.

I can't forget what I saw him do, and he knows that.

He knows what I see when I look at him, and he hates it.

"Cognac?" Valery offers after the obligatory greetings, and I nod, sitting down on a loveseat across from my brothers. It's extra cold outside tonight, and I could use a drink to warm my insides.

"So," Nikolai says after we're all seated with drinks in hand. He looks oddly tense, even though his voice is level. "As you might've heard, Ksenia Leonova died last week."

I freeze with the glass halfway to my mouth, even as my pulse jumps through the roof. Is this about Alexei? Is he about to tell me that the betrothal—

"None of us knew her," Nikolai continues evenly. "She didn't appear in society much—or so we thought. Turns out, she'd attended at least one event where our paths crossed." He fixes his gaze on Valery. "Your twenty-second birthday celebration, about five years ago."

Valery's face is impassive, as always, but I can tell he's just as confused as I am. Not Konstantin, though. Judging by his distracted expression and the way he's glancing at his phone every couple of seconds, he's heard all of this already.

"More specifically," Nikolai says. "*I* met her at your

party, Valery." He takes a deep breath and looks at each of us in turn. "I also fucked her that night."

I suck in a breath. "What? You—"

"I didn't know who she was at the time." Nikolai's tone sharpens. "I still wouldn't have known if I hadn't received a call from her friend two days ago. Turns out our one-night stand, forgettable as it was, had unintended consequences."

Valery's gaze sharpens. "Her son. He's yours, isn't he?"

I open my mouth, then close it, struck mute. Of course Valery would get there first, a split second ahead of the rest of us. Or rather just me, because once again, Konstantin doesn't display any surprise, just frowns and types something on his phone.

"Yes," Nikolai says, and this time, there's no mistaking the tension in his voice. "According to the diary Ksenia's friend found after her death, her son—Miroslav—is mine."

I open and close my mouth again, like a guppy, then down the glass of cognac in my hand. The alcohol burns a fiery path down my esophagus as my mind races to process the implications.

A child that Nikolai knew nothing about.

A boy who's both a Leonov and a Molotov.

It's unbelievable, impossible.

It was our father's dream, the reason for my betrothal to Alexei.

I begin to laugh, unable to help myself. I laugh so hard I have to set my empty glass on the table, and even then, I can't stop. Because what are the odds? What are the fucking odds? For a decade, I've been dealing with the consequences of our father's obsession with a union between our families, the "bridge over the rift" he wanted me to build with Alexei. And all along, all we had to do was get Nikolai into the same room as Ksenia. His overactive dick took care of the rest.

"No condom?" Valery asks, ignoring my hysterics, and Nikolai glares at him.

"Of course there was a fucking condom. I'm not an idiot. It was either defective or she tampered with it. I have no idea which."

I laugh harder. This is precious. God, this is so fucking precious.

Nikolai turns his lethal glare on me. "You realize this is your nephew, right? A four-year-old who's just lost his mom and now lives with his grandfather, Boris?"

The laughter dies in my throat. Boris Leonov—a man known for his cruelty. Fuck, I didn't even think about that. Nor about the fact that the boy must be massively traumatized, having lost the only parent he's ever known. "I'm sorry, I—" I cut myself off. It doesn't matter why or how or what could have been. Nothing matters but figuring out what to do next. I sit forward. "Kolya, what are you going to do?"

"I'm working on the security schematics for the Leonovs' compound," Konstantin answers in place of Nikolai, and I realize why he's been glued to his phone.

"We need to figure out how to get the boy out, first and foremost."

"And then hide him," Valery says. Clearly, the three of them are on the same wavelength, even though Valery is just learning about this, same as I am.

I twist toward him. "You mean, kidnap him?"

"I doubt the Leonovs will simply hand him over," Nikolai says.

"No, they won't." Valery cocks his head, studying Nikolai. "Do they know he's yours?"

"No," Konstantin says. "Nikolai and I took care of the friend before she could reach out to them about what she'd learned in the diary."

My chest tightens. "Took care of her how?"

"She's on her way to New Zealand with a new identity as we speak," Nikolai says.

Whew. That could've gone so much worse. Not that what's happening is good in any way. In fact, it's the exact opposite of what our father hoped to achieve. I shift my gaze from one brother to the next. "Won't this start a war with the Leonovs?"

"Not if they don't find out about it," Valery says, and it's obvious he's already thought this through. "If they don't know the boy is Nikolai's, they'll have no reason to suspect him."

"Especially if I'm not even in the country at the time of the kidnapping," Nikolai says.

Valery looks mildly curious. "Where will you be?"

"We're exploring a few alternatives," Konstantin answers again in Nikolai's stead. "Someplace remote would be best, as far from here as we can manage. That way, Nikolai can spend some time with his son, get to know him without interference."

I blink at Nikolai. "But what about the business? How will you run it if you're not in Moscow?" There's much that can be done remotely, I know, but a lot of what my brother does relies on personal contact, on the handshakes and the dinners and the hush-hush deals made behind closed doors in carefully secured rooms swept for bugs.

"That's what we're here to discuss," Nikolai says. "I've thought about this long and hard, and I only see one alternative: I have to step down temporarily." He looks at Valery and Konstantin. "The two of you will divide up my responsibilities among yourselves." He glances at me. "Unless, Alina, you would…?"

"No, no, I'm good," I say hastily. "Count me out."

Nikolai nods, unsurprised. My lack of interest in the family enterprise is well known. "Okay then." He turns to Valery. "I'm thinking you oversee the business overall, while Konstantin gets free rein with all the tech-related ventures."

Valery's eyes gleam coolly. "That works for me."

"And me," Konstantin says calmly. "I've already put some things in motion. For now, we need to figure out how to penetrate the security of the Leonovs' compound and get Nikolai's son out. I have a few ideas in that regard."

———

I'M STILL IN A STATE OF SHOCK BY THE TIME I GET HOME from the meeting, a state that persists as days turn into weeks while my brothers actively work on their plan to get Miroslav—or Slava, as everyone calls him—away from the Leonovs. It's not an easy task. Boris Leonov resides in a suburban mansion an hour's drive from Moscow, which might as well be a military fortress, and that's where the boy is staying.

Slava, not *the boy,* I correct myself. Even now, two weeks later, I'm having trouble thinking of the child as being a living, breathing person.

A person who's as much my nephew as he is Alexei's.

Each time I think about that, something inside me tightens, a strange ache filling my chest. We're now joined by blood, Alexei and I. Bonded in a way that supersedes any betrothal contract. The only way this bond would be stronger is if Slava were ours, but he's not.

He's Nikolai's.

I didn't go back to Switzerland after the meeting, even though I could have. I'm not needed here in Moscow. All the planning is unfolding without me, though I insist on being informed. That's how I know that Nikolai has purchased an old estate in the beautiful, remote mountains of Idaho—an estate that he's renovating and turning into his own fortress with furious speed. The goal is to extract Slava as quickly as possible, but it's just as important to do it right, to make sure that the Leonovs have no reason to suspect us and to have a hideaway ready for when the child is finally in our hands.

To help with the suspicion bit, I flit about town like a social butterfly. I dress up and go to parties, attend operas and ballets. I smile, laugh, and dazzle friends and opponents alike, all the while trying to process what all of this means, how our lives are going to change… how Alexei is going to react to losing his nephew so soon after his sister's death.

I don't know why I care about that. It doesn't make sense. I know what the Leonovs are like, especially Boris, the boy's grandfather. Slava will be better off with us, messed up as we are, and kidnapping is the best way to accomplish that. If Nikolai tries to go through the legal channels to claim his paternal rights, the Leonovs will hide Slava away, make him disappear. That's what we would do in their shoes. So this is the right move, the only move if we don't want Nikolai's son raised by a man known to be a monster.

Logically, I know all this. I've discussed it with Pavel, Lyudmila, and my brothers ad nauseam. However, logic takes a back seat whenever I try to imagine how Alexei will feel once our plan comes to fruition…. how he must feel already, grieving for his sister. It's a thought that wakes me up at night and snakes into my mind a dozen times each day, as intrusive and relentless as Alexei's men who keep following me.

That thought is why I agree to attend Natasha's

charity gala, even though Alexei is supposed to be there.

MY KNEES SHAKE AND TENSION BANDS MY TEMPLES AS I enter the ballroom and survey my surroundings. Everything glitters—the diamonds in women's earlobes and on their fingers, wrists, and necks, the crystal chandeliers, the stainless-steel trays deftly carried around by uniformed waiters, the mirrors lining the walls and making the event seem that much grander. I glitter too. My blue silk dress is encrusted with tiny crystals around the bodice; my smooth, shiny updo is decorated with a diamond pin.

For a second, I'm tempted to turn around and go home, to turn on my computer and disappear into the neat, predictable world of code. Yesterday, to prevent myself from obsessing about tonight's event, I pulled out my old Computer Science course materials, the ones I haven't looked at since my first semester at college but kept for some odd reason. Immediately, I got sucked back in. In some strange way, it felt like coming home, and I'm itching to get back to it, to try my hand at writing some simple programs now that working on a computer for an extended period of time doesn't make my head feel like it's exploding. In fact, coding seems much safer, headache-wise, than being here tonight, as I can feel the tension in my skull growing, threatening to transform into the familiar pain.

I should leave. Coming here was a mistake, a stupid impulse I should've squashed.

I turn to go, but Natasha has already spotted me. She waves and hurries over, and I put on a bright smile. Because that's what I do. I smile, I glitter, I pretend. Nobody, not even Natasha, knows my history with Alexei, or that I avoid him any way I can. As I should be avoiding him tonight, yet here I am, willfully putting myself in his proximity.

Maybe he won't show. That's all I can hope for right now.

Natasha and I exchange air kisses, and before I can make any kind of an excuse, she drags me into a circle of people, all of whom are eager to talk to me about tonight's cause: providing educational technology to Russia's rural areas. Every ruble donated will be converted into laptops, tablets, and other key learning tools for children from communities that may or may not have indoor toilets and running water.

It's a noble cause, and I write a big fat check from my personal account for the venture, in addition to promising that each of my brothers will do the same. Then I'm technically free to leave and I'm about to do so quickly, since I still haven't spotted Alexei, but Natasha intercepts me yet again, this time to introduce me to a few of her friends from college.

By the time I extricate myself from that conversation,

a half hour has gone by, and I'm desperate to escape. Each second that ticks by puts me closer to Alexei's arrival. Unless he won't show, but I can't count on that. I have to go, right now, before my stupid impulse leads to—

And there he is.

Our eyes meet as he cuts through the crowd like a shark through water, heading directly for me. My lungs expand, taking up the entirety of my chest and squeezing my heart into nothingness. I stop mid-stride, my feet welded to the floor, and watch helplessly as he comes toward me, a sardonic half-smile on his lips.

Why? Why did I come here? How could I have been such an idiot as to think he needed me in his grief when—

"What an unexpected pleasure," he drawls, stopping in front of me, and my mind goes completely blank, everything around us disappearing as my thoughts transform into white noise. For the past two-plus years, my PI firm has tracked him, supplying me with a steady stream of photos and videos—which I've studied as if I'll be tested on each one. And still, I'm not prepared for seeing him in person once again. All of my awareness focuses in on him, on the power and the danger and the cruel magnificence that is Alexei Leonov in a perfectly tailored black tux.

A pleasure. He said something about pleasure. Heat licks under my skin and deeper in my core, bringing with it a trickle of adrenaline. The white noise recedes, and I can once again hear the din of music and laughter, all the conversations surrounding us. With effort, I unglue my tongue from the roof of my mouth. "What are you doing here?"

Ugh, why did I just say that? Dumb, dumb, dumb. I should've—

He laughs, the soft sound mocking. "Oh, you knew I'd be here. Unless your PI firm dropped the ball?"

My pulse surges. "I don't know what you—"

He tsk-tsks. "I thought we were past such clichéd denials, Alinyonok. I stalk you, you stalk me—isn't that how our game works?"

I suck in a sharp breath. Coming here was a huge, huge mistake. What did I imagine would happen? Why did I think that by coming here and seeing him, I could somehow ease the guilt that gnaws at me whenever I think about what my brothers are planning to do to his family?

There's nothing I can do to soothe his grief over his sister's death, and I certainly can't prevent his anger over the loss of his nephew. All I've accomplished by showing up is dangling myself in front of him, showing him what he can't have—assuming he still wants it.

There's a good chance he does not.

The thought steadies me enough to say, "It pays to keep an eye on your enemy."

Another soft, derisive laugh escapes his throat. "You think I'm your enemy?"

"You're certainly not my friend."

"I could be." A peculiar gleam brightens his dark eyes. "I could be your everything."

I take a step back, my knees suddenly wobbly again.

"Look, I…" I stop and reassess what I was about to say. Given how this conversation has gone so far, my only option is radical honesty. "You're right. I knew you'd be here. I wanted to see you."

His lids lower, his gaze growing more intent. "Why?"

"I heard about Ksenia."

He flinches, ever so slightly, and I plow on, desperate to get the words out before my courage fails me. "I'm sorry. I'm really, truly sorry. I know nothing can take away this kind of pain, and I'm so sorry about that. I—" I stop and swallow thickly. "I know what it's like to lose the people closest to you."

Several micro-expressions cross his face, so fast I could be just imagining this unguarded display of emotion. When he speaks, however, his voice is detectably different. Huskier, rougher. "I know you do, Alinyonok. Thank you."

I dampen my lips. I don't know where we go from here, but it feels wrong to just walk away, to go back to our adversarial pseudo-relationship and pretend like this moment never happened.

Like I never saw him as a human being instead of the demon shadowing my life.

As I desperately rack my brain for something else to say, he beats me to it. "Have a drink with me?" he asks quietly, snatching a pair of champagne glasses off a passing waiter's tray—and I must already be drunk because I accept the glass he hands me and let him lead me to a nearby empty table.

As we sit down next to each other, I realize the insanity of what I'm doing and almost jump up to escape, but we've attracted more than a few curious glances, so I have to stay for at least a couple of minutes. We don't need all of Moscow gossiping about us. It's bad enough that I'm talking to Alexei when our families' mutual enmity is well known; sitting down and running off a second later would make the tongues wag that much harder.

For lack of anything better to do, I gulp down most of my champagne.

A wry smile tilts one corner of his mouth. "Thirsty?"

"Something like that," I mutter, and he laughs. Unlike before, it's a sound of genuine amusement, and it does something to my insides, ignites a warmth in my chest that has nothing to do with my body's typical response to him.

Not that the typical response is missing. As I cross my legs under the table, I can feel a distinct slickness in my panties, and it makes my face burn.

"So," he says, thankfully ignoring my blush. "What brings you to Moscow at this time of the year?"

I stiffen, then consciously force my muscles to relax. Shrugging as casually as I can, I take a leisurely sip of my champagne. "New Year's with family, what else?"

He tilts his head quizzically. "Why this year of all the years? I thought you were supposed to be in Switzerland."

Fuck. I should've known this would turn into an interrogation. For obvious reasons, I can't say anything about Nikolai calling a family meeting, and I don't know how else to justify cutting my ski trip short. So I just shrug again and let him draw his own conclusions —which he promptly does.

His face softens as he leans forward. "Is it because you heard about Ksenia?" His eyes search mine, and whatever he sees there makes his pupils expand, turning his irises from dark brown to a bright, intense black. His voice lowers, deepens. "Alinyonok..."

I swallow hard and avert my gaze as my face turns even hotter. Not from arousal or embarrassment, but guilt. Terrible, biting guilt that I'm letting him think this when it's so far from the truth. When my family is about to inflict another loss on his.

To compose myself, I take a sip of my drink before meeting his eyes again. "How is..." I take a breath. "How is your family coping with everything? Your sister had a son, right?"

He nods, his expression turning grim. "Slava. He's just turned four."

The guilt sinks its teeth deeper. "I'm sorry. This must be so hard for him."

Alexei's voice is tight. "I don't know. He's staying with my father, and whenever I see him, he just seems... distant. Closed off. We were close before—I was his favorite uncle—but now I can't get him to open up at all. It's as if—" He stops and waves his hand.

"Never mind. I'm sure it's just the shock of it. He'll recover in time."

"Of course he will." My brothers and I will make sure of it. I bite my lip. "You lost your mom pretty young too, didn't you?"

"I was five when she died. Complications from Ksenia's birth," he says, and even though there's no emotion in his tone, I have to fight a bizarre urge to reach over the table and hug him. I've always known that he and his siblings were raised by their father, but I never gave it much thought, except to vaguely wonder if that's why he's so ruthless… if being raised by a monster has made him one.

"That must've been equally hard for you," I say softly.

He lifts one broad shoulder in a shrug. "It was a long time ago." Picking up his glass, he leans forward. "What about you? Your loss is far more recent. How are you doing these days?"

It's my turn to flinch. To give myself a moment to recover, I down the rest of my champagne and motion to a passing waiter for more. When he places it on the table, I manage a stiff smile at Alexei. "I'm fine. It's old news for me by now as well."

"I'm glad to hear it," he says quietly and lifts his glass in a toast. His eyes lock on mine. "To those we loved and lost—may they rest in peace."

"To them," I say thickly and clink my glass against his before gulping down all of the fizzy liquid. There's a stinging behind my eyelids and a choked feeling in my throat, so I motion to another waiter, and he brings over his tray with drinks. They turn out to be vodka shots, but I don't care. I want something, anything, to drown this feeling, these memories.

If I had my pills, I'd take them, but they're at home, in my bedside drawer. I haven't needed them in months, so I stopped carrying them around.

"Two please," I tell the waiter, and he places one shot in front of me and the other in front of Alexei, who lifts his eyebrows at me but doesn't object.

"To family," I say, raising my shot glass in a toast when the waiter is gone.

"To family," Alexei echoes, touching his glass to mine.

We take the shot, and the expensive vodka goes down smoothly, with a pleasant burn. The choking sensation in my throat recedes, and I wonder, a bit hazily, if alcohol has been the answer all along.

Maybe my father had the right idea. Maybe it *is* possible to drink the pain away.

I'm about to gesture for another drink when Alexei reaches over and covers my hand with his. His palm is big and warm, his touch strangely comforting. I'm able to draw in a deeper breath, even as my pulse picks up pace, my body quickening with its usual reaction to him.

"Are you okay, Alinyonok?" he asks softly, and to my shock, I realize that I am… that the searing pain I've become conditioned to expect each time I think about my parents is only a distant ache right now, dulled either by alcohol, the passage of time, or a combination of the two. Or maybe it's none of the above. Maybe it's him. Maybe it's his touch and the warm sympathy in his dark eyes.

Maybe it's because in this moment, we're not enemies, and I don't feel so scared and alone.

"I'm okay." The words are only a faint whisper on my lips, but he hears me and his lips curve in a smile that I feel deep inside. A soft, tender smile that transforms his hard, cruelly carved features into something so breathtakingly beautiful that a tiny fissure opens in my heart… a tear that should hurt but doesn't.

He squeezes my hand lightly before interlacing our fingers together, and the ballroom once again melts away, disappearing in a foggy glow that veils my vision in every direction except the center, where he's sitting. Where he's looking at me like I am the center of *his* vision, *his* world.

"Alina?"

The female voice is soft, as is the touch on my shoulder, but it jars me all the same. Yanking my hand free, I jackknife to my feet and spin around to face Natasha.

"Hey," she says, blinking. "I didn't mean to startle you. I was calling your name, but I guess you didn't hear me." She shifts her gaze to Alexei, and a strange look flits across her face. "Alexei. Glad you could make it."

His expression is reminiscent of a thunder cloud as he stands. "So am I."

His icy tone belies his words, and my friend pales slightly. Casting an indecipherable look in my direction, she mumbles something about needing to check on the catering and hurries away before I can ask what it was that she wanted. Not that it matters. I can't stay here any longer, not after what has just happened.

"I have to go," I say tightly and beeline for the exit, weaving through the crowd as fast as my high heels allow. I ignore the voices calling to me, all the friends and acquaintances who want my attention. I walk so fast I nearly trip on the hem of my floor-length dress, and it's still not fast enough.

When I burst out through the ornate doorway into the hallway, Alexei is right behind me, his long legs catching up to me with ease.

"Alina, wait."

I pick up my pace, all but jogging toward the lobby, my breath coming fast. I can't believe I've been so stupid. I can't believe I—

"Wait, I said." A steely hand wraps around my upper arm, jerking me to a halt and spinning me around.

Before I can blink, I'm dragged to a nearby open door and into a small room that turns out to be a coat closet. Keeping his hold on me, Alexei shuts the door, isolating us from the world. Then and only then, he lets go of me.

I immediately back away. "What the fuck are you doing? I said I have to go."

"Not until we talk." Jaw clenched, he advances on me, backing me against the wall.

My heart hammers frantically, but I lift my chin to meet his gaze. "What is there to talk about?"

A dozen emotions, each darker than the next, flash across his face before he growls, "This"—and hooking one hand on my nape and the other over my hip, he slants his mouth over mine.

Chapter 21

Present Day, Location Unknown

"That shouldn't have happened," I say, my face burning at the memory of what went down that evening.

Alexei arches his eyebrows. "Which part? You pretending to be oh-so sympathetic about my sister, all the while knowing you and your brothers were about to steal her son? Or us—"

"I wasn't pretending."

The admission hangs between us, suspended in the tense atmosphere like a broken leaf in a spiderweb. I don't know why I said it. Why should I care what he thinks about my motivations? If anything, it's better if he believes hate, and only hate, drives me. Which is the case. It has to be. So what if it felt like we had a real connection for that brief moment nine months ago?

It doesn't change what I did after that night.

It doesn't change the way he responded.

And it certainly doesn't change where we are today or how many deaths are on my conscience.

Chapter 22

9 Months Earlier, Moscow

Our lips crash together like rogue waves colliding, all violence and pent-up fury. He's angry with me, and I'm angry with myself, with this weakness of mine that propels me toward a man I should do everything in my power to escape. I didn't have to be here tonight. I didn't have to be anywhere near him, yet I came of my own volition. And not just to offer my condolences.

I came to see *him*.

After years of encountering him only in pictures and videos, I've grown hungry for this. For him. For feeling like I'm not just surviving, but living.

His tongue sweeps into my mouth as my nails dig into his skull, my fingers convulsively gripping his hair, and my eyes squeeze shut as my body catches fire, instant arousal drenching my underwear and hardening my nipples. Fuck, yes, I'm hungry. I'm starved for the taste of him, the feel of him, the way he ignites every cell of my being.

I'm hungry, and I'm angry, and I feel like I'm going to explode from the heat building inside me… from the desperate need to burrow into him until we're so close that it's impossible to tell where one begins and the other ends.

He groans low in his throat, and his kiss grows rougher, his teeth nipping at my lower lip, his fingers digging into my flesh with bruising force. It should hurt, should frighten me, the violence of his desire, but it just adds to the boiling cauldron inside me, intensifying everything I'm feeling to the nth degree. I taste blood as my teeth sink into *his* lip in retaliation, and I don't know if it's his blood or mine—nor do I care. I'm burning, dying, and at the same time, I'm violently, incandescently alive. I can hear each thudding heartbeat in my chest, feel every breath he steals from me… smell the heat rising between us, dark and forest-wild, edged with musk and man and something ineffably appealing.

Breathing raggedly, he breaks the kiss, only to grip my hair in his fist and pull on it, arching my head back to press his hot, wet mouth to the vulnerable bend of my throat. His teeth graze over my skin, and then he sucks on it, sending erotic chills down my arm and wrenching a series of moans from my throat. At the same time, he bunches his other fist in my skirt and pulls it up, causing cool air to wash over my newly exposed thighs.

It's like my eighteenth-birthday party all over again, only I'm no longer that naïve, anxious girl—and he's no longer inclined to be patient with me. I can feel the raging hunger in his touch, in the demanding hardness of his body. The thick bulge of his erection throbs against my stomach, hot and hard even through the layers of our clothing, and my insides clench on an answering empty ache, on an acute craving for something I've never known.

Sensing that, he pulls back and slips his hand between my legs to palm my sex through the wet silk of my thong. A low, deep growl rumbles in his throat as I gasp, my eyes flying open. "I fucking knew it." He lifts his head to pin me with a dark, burning gaze. "You still want me. The moment I touch you, you're fucking soaked with it."

I flush scarlet, my mind clearing for a moment, but he bends his head to ravish my mouth again, and I forget all about embarrassment and shame as a flood of sensations overwhelms me once more. Those skilled fingers of his are already underneath my thong, parting my slick folds and finding my clit to start a wicked, mind-bending rhythm. *Number three,* I think hazily as he sweeps his tongue over mine, stroking, claiming, invading. *He's going to give me orgasm number three.*

And he does. He's still kissing me as sparks light my vision, the pleasure blinding in its intensity. The climax roars through me, awakening every nerve ending in my body, making me convulse against him with a gasping cry. Only he doesn't stop this time, doesn't remove his hand from between my legs or lift his head to let me catch my breath. Instead, he presses the heel of his palm against my swollen flesh, intensifying the aftershocks, and kisses me so hard I taste blood again.

The twin sensations—pain and pleasure—are so potent I almost miss the hard push of his finger into me and the accompanying slight burn. Almost but not quite. Instinctively, I tense, and the burn intensifies, as does an unfamiliar feeling of being stretched and penetrated. My breath catches in my throat, and I grip his shoulders as a spear of rational thinking pierces the sensual fog in my brain.

I shouldn't be doing this.

I shouldn't be here, with him.

Alexei must feel me stiffen because he raises his head to stare down at me, onyx eyes filled with dark hunger. "You're so small, even for a virgin," he whispers roughly, and the hot blush washes over me again, making the very roots of my hair feel like they're on fire. His finger is still inside me, penetrating me, but it no longer hurts, though it still feels invasive. Worse yet, I can feel myself getting even wetter, and I know he can feel it too.

"Don't fight it, Alinyonok. Let me in." His eyes burn into mine as his thumb circles my clit at the same time as the stinging stretch returns. He's probing at my entrance with a second finger, I comprehend vaguely as a wave of dizziness sweeps over me, along with the realization that I've stopped breathing.

Tell him to stop. Now. Before it's too late.

Except I can't form the words fast enough. He kisses me again, stealing what little oxygen remains in my lungs, and I melt against him despite the growing discomfort between my legs. Two fingers are way too much, the stinging stretch threatening to turn into real pain, but his thumb is still doing that circling thing, and there's just enough pleasure to confuse my senses and muddle my thoughts. I'm lost in him, utterly absorbed in the sensations he's evoking in my body, and even the sharp pinch of pain as he pushes his fingers deeper into me isn't enough to make me pull away—especially since he curls those fingers, pressing on a spot that brings back that sweet, agonizing tension, sending me barreling toward another peak.

With a muffled cry against his lips, I come, the second orgasm exploding through me. My inner muscles clamp down on his invading fingers, causing another pinch of pain, along with a series of aftershocks. My body is still spasming weakly when he pulls his fingers out, and I hear the metallic hiss of a zipper being lowered before my thong is ripped away with a sharp tug. Dazed, I open my eyes as he stops kissing me and lifts his head.

He's breathing hard and his jaw is tightly clenched, his sharp cheekbones spotted with color as he raises his hand to look at it. His fingers are colored red—the same fingers that were just inside me. Red with my blood, I realize with growing alarm as he drops his hand and meets my gaze, his eyes coal-black and filled with terrifying possessiveness. "Fucking mine," he breathes roughly. "All mine."

And before I can respond, he's kissing me again. Kissing me and lifting me up the wall by hooking his hands under my thighs and opening them wide. His suit pants rub against my bare inner thighs as he presses his lower body against mine, and something big, smooth, and hard prods between my folds, pushing a few millimeters into my sore, swollen opening. His cock, I realize with a jolt. It's way too big, much bigger than his fingers, but pinned against the wall as I am, there's nothing I can do to stop the penetration, to slow it down. Panic surges through me, along with the full understanding of what's happening, and I manage to turn my head, tearing my lips away from his devouring kiss as I push on his shoulders. "Alexei, please." My voice shakes. "Please, st—"

With a squeak of hinges, the door opens, and Alexei stiffens as Vankov steps into the room. Assessing the situation in a flash, my bodyguard draws his gun with lightning speed and points it at Alexei.

"Step back from Alina Vladimirovna. Now!"

A low growl of frustration vibrates in Alexei's chest, and murder glitters in his eyes as he returns his gaze to my face, not moving an inch. "Order him to leave," he says through clenched teeth. "Tell him this is what you want, and that he should go."

But I don't want this. I can't, not with the panic tightening my throat. I know exactly what Vankov is seeing—me pinned against the wall like some cheap whore in an alley, with my dress hiked up and Alexei between my parted legs—and horrified embarrassment extinguishes all remnants of desire. All I feel now is the soreness deep inside, where Alexei broke my hymen with his fingers, and the enormous pressure of his cock pushing against my entrance, threating to tear me apart. The pain is not what scares me, though. It's everything else.

It's knowing that once we do this, there's no going back… that we might've already reached the point of no return.

"Let me go." My ragged whisper is meant only for Alexei's ears. "Please, let me go."

A muscle flexes violently in his jaw as he stares down at me. "Or what? You'll have him shoot me?"

"Step back from her! Now!" Vankov's tone is sharper, more agitated. Out of the corner of my eye, I see my other two bodyguards appear behind him, and I want to die on the spot.

My face must reflect my thoughts because Alexei's features tighten further, and without another word, he lowers me to my feet and zips himself up in one quick, furious motion. He doesn't step back, however. Instead, he props one hand on the wall and leans over me. Lifting his other hand, he presses his bloodied fingertips to my lips, imprinting them with red as he says in a low, hard voice, "I will send a car for you tomorrow night. You will come. If you don't, you will regret it."

With that, he pushes off the wall and strides past my bodyguards to disappear into the hallway.

———

THE COPPER TASTE IS STILL ON MY LIPS AS I GET INTO MY limo, and I can feel the soreness of my broken hymen deep inside. I have no idea what to do, especially in light of Alexei's invitation/threat. What did he mean, I will regret it? What I regret right now is going to Natasha's event and everything that followed. It's like I temporarily went insane.

Obviously, I have no intention of getting into any car he sends. My insanity doesn't extend that far. But what will he do when I don't show? Maybe I should tell my brothers what happened, warn them just in case. But no. If they knew that Alexei nearly fucked me in a coat closet and is now threatening me, they'd have no choice but to go after him, and that would be the worst timing ever.

Tomorrow morning, Nikolai is leaving Moscow for the foreseeable future. He's flying to America to prepare his new Idaho compound for Slava's arrival in three weeks' time. If my stupidity were to screw that up, I'd never forgive myself.

I catch Vankov's eyes in the rearview mirror before leveling a hard look at the other two guards. "If so much as a word about this incident gets out—and especially if it gets back to my brothers—all three of you will be fired on the spot. Understand?"

All three of them nod, their faces impassive. They know it's not an idle threat. They're on my payroll, have been ever since I received my inheritance a few months after my parents' deaths. My brothers objected at first, claiming it was their duty to protect me, but I stood my ground. What did it matter to them, I argued, as long as I had proper security detail? So they gave in, however reluctantly, and I've been my bodyguards' official employer ever since, ensuring that they're loyal to me first and foremost.

Appeased, I lean back against the seat and focus on taking deep breaths to calm the frantic racing of my heart and ease the tension squeezing my temples. I need to figure out what to do, how to fix this mess I've created, and I can't do that if I'm curled up in bed with another debilitating headache. I've been doing so much better in recent months, have felt so much stronger, yet here I am, about to unravel again.

No, fuck that. I'm not letting it happen. Clearly, Alexei is my kryptonite, in more ways than one, so there's only one rational solution.

I have to take myself out of his orbit, get as far away from him as I can. Maybe I can go to Switzerland for a proper ski trip, or join Natasha on her upcoming vacation in Thailand. Then again, what if Alexei follows me there to do whatever it is he's threatening? It's not like he doesn't have a private jet and an army of thugs to do his bidding. If anything, I'd be making it easier for him to steal me or whatever he intends. What

I need is to completely fall off his radar for a time, so he'll forget about what happened tonight and—

I sit up, electrified. Of course! The perfect getaway has been in front of me all along.

Nikolai's new compound. It's the closest I can get to disappearing while still remaining on the same planet.

This is it. This is the solution to all my problems.

When Nikolai leaves tomorrow, I will go with him—and Alexei will never find me.

Chapter 23

Present Day, Location Unknown

"You shouldn't have run," Alexei says as a gust of wind brings a cool spray of ocean water to the table. Or maybe it's the beginnings of rain. The waves are intensifying, the yacht rocking harder. A zigzag of lightning bisects the rapidly darkening sky, followed by a bone-rattling boom of thunder. Soon, it'll be too dangerous to sit here. I, however, am far more afraid of what awaits me below the deck, in the bedroom Alexei intends for us to share. I interlace my hands on the table to steady them as he continues. "We could've had this meal in a nice restaurant in Moscow."

And with a lot less blood spilled. He doesn't say that, but he doesn't have to.

"What were you planning to do?" I ask, doing my best to keep my voice calm as I pour myself a glass of water from a crystal pitcher on the table. My mouth is dry, and the caviar sandwich I consumed feels like it's stuck halfway down my throat. "If I'd stayed in

Moscow, what would you have done when I didn't get into your car?"

A twisted smile plucks at his lips. "What do you think?"

I drain half of the water in the glass before setting it down. "I think you're a monster capable of anything."

"You know me so well."

His dry tone makes me wince internally. Because he's right. I don't know him. At least not nearly as well as he knows me. All of my stalking of him was surface level, designed to keep me apprised of his whereabouts, whereas he's delved into every area of my life, no matter how private. I regret that now, not getting to know him better before, when the stakes were much lower. Now he's my captor, and I have no idea what his weaknesses are, how I can manipulate him into granting me freedom.

The dark, powerful man sitting in front of me is a mystery, a puzzle. All I know is that he wants me and has gone to incredible—and terrible—lengths to claim me. And all because... what? I'm beautiful as decreed by some arbitrary societal standard?

"Is it a status thing for you?" I ask, cocking my head. Maybe it's not too late for me to try to get to know him, to understand what drives him.

His eyebrows furrow. "Is what a status thing?"

"Me. The betrothal. This whole obsession of yours." I steady the pitcher as it begins to slide toward the edge of the table, aided by a puddle of condensation and a tall wave tilting the yacht. "You said it's because of my looks, but Moscow is full of gorgeous women. So is it because I'm a Molotov? Do you want me because I'm both decorative *and* rich?"

As far as I can tell, that's about the only unique thing about me. Beauty is nothing special in our circles; throw a rock at a party, and it'll bounce off a supermodel. But as a rule, those women don't have much to offer beyond their perfect bodies and symmetrical faces. I do. I have billions in assets and the kinds of connections only generational power can bring. The Leonovs don't need that, strictly speaking—they have enough power and wealth of their own—but having me would still be a coup for Alexei.

I'm arm candy that can't be bought, and that makes me the ultimate status symbol, a prize worthy of a man who has everything.

Alexei's eyes narrow. "Is that what—"

"May I clear away the table, sir?"

An unfamiliar woman's voice speaking Russian startles me into looking up. A short, middle-aged woman with straight, shoulder-length black hair is standing by the table, an apron wrapped around her waist and a waiter's cart at her side.

"Yes, thank you, Vika," Alexei says, then pauses and arches an eyebrow at me. "Unless you're still hungry, Alinyonok?"

As much as I'd like to stretch out this meal for as long as I can, with the storm, it's only a matter of minutes before all the plates start sliding off the table and the food goes flying. Reluctantly, I shake my head. "I'm done."

The woman—Vika—swiftly stacks all the dishes onto the cart and wheels it toward the nose of the yacht, where the kitchen must be.

"Thank you," I call after her belatedly. "Everything was delicious!"

It doesn't hurt to get on Alexei's employees' good side.

She turns her head, flashing a smile that softens her angular face. "It was my pleasure," she calls back before pushing the cart around the corner and disappearing from sight.

I return my attention to Alexei, hoping to continue the conversation, but he's already on his feet. "Shall we?" he asks, coming around the table to extend a hand as another bolt of lightning flashes closer. My pulse kicks up, its roar nearly drowning out the ensuing boom of thunder.

This is it.

My reprieve, such as it was, is over.

Chapter 24

5 Months Earlier, Idaho

A reprieve. A refuge. That's what Nikolai's remote mountain estate is supposed to be. It's a timeout from my regular life, a safe place where I don't have to worry about Alexei. So why do I feel so restless, so uneasy? I can't stop thinking about him, about what happened in that coat closet, and it's slowly driving me mad.

Unsettled, I take one last drag on my joint and put it out before heading out of the woods. The pot has been keeping the headaches at bay for the most part, so I haven't had to resort to anything stronger. I don't know why I'm having the headaches at all; I can't imagine a more relaxing place than Nikolai's new compound.

My brother's ultra-modern mansion is perched on a cliff, with Instagram-worthy mountain views all around. Despite May being right around the corner, we've just had a snowfall, and fresh powder crunches under my boots as I circle around the house to the front door. The air is crisp and pine-scented, so cool and fresh it almost hurts my lungs. Then again, maybe that's what the problem is. The smell reminds me of Alexei and everything I'm here to escape.

Inhaling another lungful, I open the door and traipse into the house, where I hang up my coat and change out of my boots into a pair of clean shoes—high heels, because even here, I feel more comfortable wearing my glossy shield. Savory smells waft from the kitchen—Pavel is cooking dinner—and a child's high-pitched voice alerts me to my nephew's presence in the living room.

My mood lifts instantly, and I smile as I head over there. Slava has quickly become my favorite person. A tiny clone of Nikolai, the child is shy and reticent, especially around his father, but I love having him around. After the first few weeks, during which he understandably regarded us all with deep suspicion, he's begun to warm up to me, as well as to Pavel and Lyudmila. Nikolai is the exception; for some reason, the two of them can't find a common language—partially because he insists we speak to the boy in English, so he can adjust to his new life in America. Personally, I don't think that's nearly as important as Slava accepting his father, but Nikolai doesn't listen to me. We don't exactly have the warmest relationship these days.

I find Slava in the living room, as expected, but instead of Lyudmila, who's taken on the role of his nanny, Nikolai is with him. My brother is pacing in front of the couch where Slava is sitting, trying to get his son to repeat some English words after him—and failing miserably. Slava is staring at him blankly, stubbornly disinterested. I'm not surprised. Slava has been ignoring my attempts to teach him the language as well.

"Maybe we should get him an American tutor," I say in English, walking over to sit on a loveseat across from the couch. "He might respond better to someone who doesn't actually speak his native tongue."

Nikolai stops pacing and gives me a cool look. "We don't need a stranger coming and going at all times."

"What if it were a live-in person?"

He snorts. "Even worse."

"Why?" Wait, why am I pushing for this? I don't care if Slava learns English or not. That's important to my brother, not to me. "Never mind. Forget it."

Perversely, *that* seems to convince Nikolai of the merit of my idea. "Actually…" He glances at his son, who's now regarding him warily. "We could place an ad in a local paper, see if any teachers from the town bite. If we keep it offline and low key, it should be safe enough."

I shrug. "If you want." It's his call either way. I just want Slava to settle in and accept us as his new family, and if learning English from a tutor facilitates that, I'm all for it.

Catching Slava's gaze, I give him a warm smile and mouth, *"Privet." Hi* in Russian.

Slava doesn't smile back—he never does when Nikolai is around—but I can feel him relax a little. In many ways, we're still strangers to him, and the artificial language barrier doesn't help. We made sure his abduction was as trauma-free as possible—he was stolen in the middle of the night with the help of a little child-safe tranquilizer, so from his perspective, he just woke up here—but that doesn't negate the fact that he's been ripped away from everything and everyone he knows. I wish I could get Nikolai to understand that and just be kind and patient, but whenever my brother is around his son, he's stiff and harsh, seemingly lacking in all empathy.

It's like our father's ghost has inhabited his body, ruining whatever chance Nikolai had at building rapport with his own son. Maybe as punishment for his murder.

I shiver as the dark memories press in, and it takes everything I have to maintain my warm, friendly smile. It's not Slava's fault his new family is nearly as messed up as his old. He's better off with us than with the Leonovs—I have to believe that—but I was hoping Nikolai's son would genuinely be happy here. So far, that's not the case.

I stand, approach the couch, and extend a hand to my nephew. "Come, Slavochka," I say in Russian, ignoring my brother's scowl. "I have a new game I want to show you."

And as Slava eagerly jumps off the couch and wraps his small palm around mine, my heart squeezes with a strange, piercing ache… one that, for some reason, makes me think of a man who's nowhere near here.

A man I have escaped.

Chapter 25

Present Day, Location Unknown

No escape.

The words drum in my mind as Alexei leads me down the stairs to our cabin, his hand wrapped securely around my elbow—ostensibly to keep me from falling as the ever-growing waves rock the yacht. But in reality, it's to make sure I don't do something as foolish as running. I know he can sense the panic-driven urge within me, hear my fast, shallow breaths.

This is it.

After more than a decade, our cat-and-mouse game is coming to an end.

As we reach the bottom of the stairs, a clap of thunder makes me jump, and he glances at me, eyebrows raised. "Are you afraid of thunderstorms, Alinyonok?"

I'm afraid of you and what you're going to do to me. The words dance on the tip of my tongue, but I swallow them down. I don't want him to know how much of a coward I am, how I am selfishly wishing that despite everything, my brothers would come and find me.

But Alexei knows, of course. His eyes shine black as he stops in front of the cabin door. "Are you regretting our bargain?" His tone is soft, mocking as he stares down at me. He knows the answer—the only answer I can give.

"No." How can I, when it was the only way? When the alternative meant that Nikolai would lose his son and, most likely, his life? Not to mention what could've happened to Chloe, Pavel, and Lyudmila.

My only regret is that I hadn't stepped forward and made the trade sooner, before the bloodbath that took the lives of so many of my brother's men.

CHAPTER 26

1 DAY EARLIER, IDAHO

I advance on horseback to the next boss and jab it with my sword. The creature shrieks and falls, but instead of blood spurting from its chest wound, its head falls off.

Oops. That isn't supposed to happen.

I jot down the error, so I can review my code tomorrow, when my mind is fresh. I'm still trying to master C++, but thanks to the latest development tools, the graphics of the video game I'm creating look amazing, and I've got one boss battle down so far. I'm sure my former Computer Science classmates would laugh at my pitiful efforts, but I'm proud of how far I've come in the past few months.

It helps that besides enjoying gorgeous nature, there's little to do in Nikolai's remote mountain estate. Well, little to do besides obsess about Alexei. If I didn't have my game to work on, I would probably go insane. As is—

The sound of something crashing onto the floor reaches my hearing, followed by a woman's moans.

I roll my eyes. Of course. Nikolai is fucking Chloe again, most likely in his office. Poor girl. From the moment my brother saw her application for the tutor position, he's been scarily obsessed with her, to the point that I've felt compelled to warn her about Molotov men and their dangerous fixations. Not that it's helped. It's only been a couple of months, but he's already bullied her into marrying him.

I do my best to tune out the sex sounds, but it's impossible. Even muffled by the walls, the noises reach me, reminding me of everything I've been trying to forget. Like the fact that Alexei is now in the United States—that for weeks, he's been circling ever closer. My PI firm hasn't been able to keep track of all of his movements, but I know he's out there. I've seen the emails in Nikolai's inbox, talking about the encroaching threat. Despite our best efforts to throw the Leonovs off our scent, Alexei suspects my family of being involved in Slava's abduction, and he's looking for Nikolai… and for me. My brothers have tried to keep me in the dark about it, as if I were a child, but I'm not. I know what Alexei is capable of, and I know he doesn't give up.

Ugh. There I go again, thinking about him, worrying, obsessing. I guess my brother isn't the only Molotov around here who fixates on things.

With effort, I refocus on my game, editing a few

clunky lines of code to make them more elegant. I get so absorbed in my task that when my laptop screen suddenly goes dark, I just stare at it in disbelief for a moment. Of all the fucking times for my computer to crash… When was the last time I hit "save"?

I expect the laptop to reboot on its own within seconds, but it doesn't. Frustrated, I jab the power button.

Nothing.

What the hell?

I check to make sure it's plugged in, and it is. There's no way it could've run out of juice.

On instinct, I grab my phone from where it's lying face down on my desk.

The screen is black, unresponsive. It won't start, no matter what I do.

My stomach drops, a chill permeating my entire body.

One of my electronics dying is an accident. Two is a pattern. A pattern that can only mean—

A banging on my bedroom door sends adrenaline surging through my veins. I jump to my feet.

"Alina!" Pavel's voice is tense. "Open up."

I'm already hurrying over. Heart pounding, I jerk the door open and see Pavel there, along with Lyudmila, who's holding a sleepy-looking Slava in her arms.

"The three of you need to get down to the safe room," Pavel says grimly. He's speaking English, likely so Slava won't understand. "I've lost contact with the guards."

My adrenaline levels skyrocket. "You have to get Nikolai and Chloe. They're in his office."

"Already on it." He steps over to Nikolai's office and bangs on the door as Lyudmila hurries down the hallway to the stairs. I run after her, ignoring the discomfort of doing so in high heels. I didn't change after dinner, so I'm still wearing my red evening gown —a small mercy, as I could've easily been in my sleepwear by now.

The safe room is underneath the garage, and both Lyudmila and I know the code. Since she's got Slava, I punch the numbers into a small gray box on the wall. With a faint hiss, a square piece of the floor near us lifts, separating from the rest, and a smaller square in the middle slides to the side, revealing a handle. I tug on it, and the heavy metal door lifts, hinging toward me to reveal a fold-out ladder underneath. I drop to my knees and jab a button on the side of the ladder, unfolding it into the space below—a bunker the size of a studio apartment, stocked with enough supplies to house several people for six weeks.

As I do this, I don't let myself think of who or what is out there. I just focus on getting us to safety and ignoring the sick feeling in my stomach.

"You go first," I tell Lyudmila, grabbing Slava from her. My hands shake, but my voice is steady. "He'll climb down to you."

She does as I say, and Slava squirms in my arms,

now fully awake. "What's going on?" he pipes up in Russian, his big eyes wide and fearful. "Why are we here? Lyudmila said it's just a drill, but what's a drill? Is it a bad thing?"

"No, no, Slavochka, a drill is not a bad thing." I shift most of his weight onto my left hip and pat his back reassuringly. The feel of him, small yet sturdy and warm, helps me maintain my outward calm. "We're just practicing what to do if there's ever a problem, okay?"

He blinks. "What kind of problem?"

"Oh, you know..." I rack my brain for something that wouldn't frighten an almost-five-year-old, but he beats me to it.

"Like if a supervillain comes?"

I beam at him. "That's right." Thank God for comic books and little boys' obsession with them. "So we know what to do in case a supervillain comes."

Slava puffs up. "I can beat him. I'm strong, like Superman."

"Yes, you are." God, this child is precious. I can't believe I didn't know him for the first four years of his life. And if I feel this way, I can't imagine how Nikolai is handling that devastating knowledge—especially now that he and Slava are growing closer.

"Ready!" Lyudmila calls from below.

I carefully set Slava down on his feet and crouch in front of him. "Part of the drill is climbing down this ladder. Do you think you're up for it?"

He bobs his head. "I know how to climb."

"Okay, good." I squeeze his thin shoulder. "Now go.

Be fast but careful, okay? Lyudmila is waiting for you below."

He clambers down the ladder like a monkey, and a few seconds later, Lyudmila shouts that she has him. Relief surges through me, and I hurry down the ladder as well, descending into the safe room.

Lyudmila grabs me by the arm as soon as my feet touch the ground. "None of the monitors work," she whispers in my ear. Stepping back, she nods toward the wall of screens that are supposed to display camera views from outside but currently show only static.

Fuck. My pulse leaps higher as I remember my dead phone and computer.

It's an EMP. It has to be, even though the lights in the house never went out. Konstantin, tech-savvy paranoiac that he is, worried about the possibility of such an attack, so our key power lines are buried underground and hardened with metal casings, and our backup generator resides in a Faraday cage. But our phones, laptops, cameras, and drones—all the electronics that were out in the open—must've gotten fried by the electromagnetic pulse, and I can think of only one enemy of ours who'd have access to such an advanced weapon.

The Leonovs.

Alexei has found us.

A distant pop of gunfire makes me jump.

Fuck. There's no longer any doubt.

This *is* an attack.

It's real.

It's happening.

I begin to pace in a futile effort to control my anxiety. In addition to a tiny but fully equipped kitchen, the bunker boasts a king-sized bed, two futons, a small bathroom, and a pantry. Theoretically, there's plenty of space, but I feel claustrophobic, trapped like a rat in a cage.

Only minutes must pass before Chloe appears, but it feels like an eternity. She climbs down the ladder and closes the ceiling hatch behind her. She also hasn't changed out of her evening wear, and her white gown glows under the bright ceiling lights, as does her smooth, olive-toned complexion. In general, she's got that dewy, flushed look of someone who's just had amazing sex, and for a moment, I feel a sharp, illogical pang of jealousy.

But no. That's stupid. I don't want sex. I don't want love and marriage, especially with a man as dangerous and obsessive as my brother. I just want to be left alone.

As soon as Chloe is on the ground, Slava runs to her. I'm not surprised. She's now by far his favorite person—undoubtedly another reason Nikolai has decided to force her into marriage. Not that she doesn't have other great qualities besides her affinity for children. I like her a lot too; we've become friends in recent weeks.

"Sit, please," Lyudmila hisses under her breath as I pace past her, so I force myself to stop and take a seat on the futon across from the bed where Chloe has sat down with Slava. He's on her lap, hugging her neck, and I feel another irrational surge of jealousy—this time, because I want to be the one holding him, deriving comfort from his small, warm weight.

"Lyudmila told him it's just a drill," I say in English, keeping my voice low. I hope Slava doesn't understand. Thanks to Chloe, my nephew now knows a bunch of words and a few basic sentences in English, but he's still far from fluent. "He's taking it well, don't you think?"

Chloe swallows visibly and glances up as more gunfire sounds in the distance. Her voice is only marginally unsteady. "Yeah. He's doing great."

Whereas I'm a nervous wreck, and so is she. She's tapping her bare foot on the floor, the sound pounding at my brain like a hammer.

"Please don't do that," I say, and she stops, only to begin chewing on her bottom lip.

Lyudmila, who's sitting on the other futon, gives me a reproving look. She's as pale as I must be, but she's holding it together, even though Pavel is out there, in danger, same as Nikolai.

Same as Alexei, if he's behind it all.

I take a breath and try to get a hold of myself—without much success. My head feels like it's been gripped in a vise, one that tightens more with each passing second. I don't know what's going on out there, but I can imagine. We have a couple of dozen guards patrolling the perimeter, all of them highly trained, and Nikolai and Pavel are each worth at least a dozen men.

But they're still human, still fallible. If the attackers have come with a big enough force—

More distant gunfire. Chloe flinches, hugging Slava tighter, and Lyudmila jumps. My neck and shoulders feel like they've been fused with metal as I sit there rigidly, trying not to move.

Tap. Tap. Tap. Tap. Tap. Tap.

Dammit. Chloe is tapping her foot on the floor again. I try to focus on something else, anything else, but the sound is driving me insane, melding as it does with the frantic rhythm of my heartbeat and the throbbing at my temples.

I shoot an acid glare her way, but she doesn't see it. I guess I have to say it. "Stop it, Chloe."

My tone is sharper than I intended, and her head jerks up, her big brown eyes startled. "Sorry about that." She shifts Slava from one knee to the other. "I'm just worried for them."

She's worried? My entire body is a raw, exposed nerve, my stomach knotted so tightly I might throw up.

The Leonovs have found us.

I'm almost certain it's Alexei's forces out there.

Lyudmila gives me a sympathetic look, and I drag in a strained breath. We're in a safe room, but I don't feel the least bit safe. How can I, when there is a war going on above us? When men might be bleeding, dying? When I suspect it's at least partially my fault?

Tap. Tap. Tap. Tap. Tap. Tap.

I jackknife to my feet. "Can you just fucking stop?"

Under different circumstances, I would be

sympathetic to Chloe's distress, but my ribcage feels like it's folding in on itself, and my headache is worsening by the second. I had another bad episode recently, one that required me to resort to my pills, and I'm still not entirely over it. Each day, I battle the urge to take a pill or two... or ten. It's so tempting to just swallow the painkillers and float away, to forget the ever-present fear and doubt.

Have I endangered my brother and his new family by hiding out with them?

Would Alexei have been as determined to locate Nikolai's compound if he didn't suspect that I am here?

Chloe tenses, and I can tell she's about to snap back at me when Lyudmila turns to me. Despite her pallor, her voice is calm, soothing as she says in Russian, "It's not the girl's fault. She's just afraid for Nikolai."

Of course she is. I can't blame her. I'm terrified for my brother, and for Pavel and all the guards. *And for Alexei.*

The throbbing in my temples sharply intensifies, and I sink back onto the futon, breathing shallowly. It's so stupid to think about that, about the danger to Alexei when *he* is the danger, but I can't help it. My hand shakes as I shove it through my hair before smoothing it down the front of my dress.

God, I'm such a fucking mess.

The futon compresses next to me, and I look up to find Chloe perched there, sans Slava, who's now sitting by himself on the bed, surveying us curiously.

"Are you okay?" she asks in a low voice.

I stare at her in silence, and she continues, undeterred. "Is something else going on? You seem unusually agitated—not that you don't have good reason to be."

I'm about to reply, but then I shake my head. She doesn't know anything about me and Alexei, and this isn't the time to delve into it. Besides, even though I'm convinced it's Alexei out there, that hasn't been officially confirmed. It could still be some other enemy of ours—or even Chloe's. "It's nothing," I say tightly. "I'm getting a bad headache, that's all."

Sympathy fills her warm brown gaze. My headaches—that she knows about. She covers my hand with hers, her slender palm warm on my frozen skin. "Do you have your medication?"

"No."

Her gaze immediately strays to the ladder leading up to the garage.

"Don't even think about it," I say sharply. "If I want it, I'll get it myself. But neither one of us should—"

A deafening explosion shakes the room, making the ceiling light flicker and sending bits of plaster raining down. My pulse leaps, icy terror coating my insides. On instinct, I jump to my feet, and so do Chloe and Lyudmila. On the bed, Slava's eyes are wide with fear. Our security drill lie has to be less believable by the second.

I start toward him, only to have Chloe beat me there. Grabbing him, she settles him on her hip, and before I can say anything, I hear his thin, high-pitched voice speaking English, as per Chloe's teachings over the past couple of months.

"Mama Chloe, where's Papa? I don't like this. I want him with me."

She hugs him tighter, like the adoptive parent she's become. "Me too, darling. Me too. But don't worry. It'll be okay. Your daddy will be here soon. We just need to wait."

Her words are meant to be reassuring, and maybe to Slava, they are. All I can think about, however, is that a potentially lethal blast just went off. That at this very moment, someone I care about might be out there, lying in pieces. It could be Nikolai. It could be Pavel. It could be—oh, God—Alexei.

I have to do something. If it is Alexei's forces out there, I can't let this go on. I have to stop this. I have to—

Lyudmila steps up to me. Wrapping her arm around my shoulders, she bends her head toward me and murmurs in Russian, "Don't even think about it. You'll only get in the way. Alexei is here for the boy, and your brother is not going to give him up, you know that. Whatever you think you can do, you can't. Neither can I. The best thing we can do is stay here, where my husband and your brother don't need to worry about us."

She's both right and wrong. Unlike Chloe, she knows about the betrothal, but she doesn't realize that Alexei and I have this whole other history between us, that Slava may not be the main reason Alexei is here, *if* he's here. What she *is* right about is that it would be stupid to leave the safety of this bunker, to get in the way of whatever is going on above us. Lyudmila and I are both pretty good shots, thanks to Pavel's training, but we've never been in actual combat. We'd be a liability out there, as surely as—

"What do you think caused that?" Chloe bursts out. Realizing she's scaring Slava, she hugs him tighter and continues in a steadier voice. "The explosion, I mean. Do you think—"

Oddly, her panic calms me a bit. "Could be an RPG," I say, covering my terror with a flat, emotionless tone of voice as I step out of Lyudmila's hold. I have to pull myself together, for everybody's sake. "They could've launched it at the garage to take out our vehicles and eliminate the option of escape. Either that, or they manually planted some explosives at the garage entrance—which would mean they're already here, at the house."

To my surprise, the words coming out of my mouth make some sort of sense. I try to think rationally, to further analyze the situation.

If they are at the house, we need to prepare.

Shoving down the emotions threatening to choke me, I head over to the wall of monitors.

Chloe is apparently on the same wavelength because she asks, "Are there any guns down here? I've been to a shooting range a few times, so I can—" She stops as she sees me press my palm against the wall. It slides away, revealing an extensive weapons collection.

"My brother has foreseen everything," I say as I reach in and pick up a Glock. This is one of the many armories hidden throughout the house. Nikolai showed them all to me when we first arrived. "They're unlikely to find this room anytime soon, but if they do, we'll be ready," I continue as I load the gun.

Chloe's face is ashen as she sets Slava down and starts toward the armory, only to have the child wrap his arms around her legs. "I want Daddy." Tears enter his voice as he tips his head back to stare up at her. "Where is he?"

My chest tightens painfully. I'm about to go reassure him, but Chloe is already on it. She pats his dark hair, her expression soft and her voice only slightly distressed. "I don't know, darling, but I'm sure we'll see him soon. For now, we just need to be prepared, okay? So your daddy knows we didn't fail this drill and that we can take care of ourselves—that we're all strong, like Superman."

Slava lets out a sniff but releases Chloe's legs, allowing her to move.

"Good boy," she murmurs and glances at Lyudmila, who's now arming herself as well. For whatever reason, that triggers Chloe again. Her voice jumps in volume. "What the fuck are we doing down here? We should be out there, helping them!" Catching herself, she modulates her tone and reaches for a gun. "Maybe one of us can stay down here to watch over—"

Another blast reverberates through the safe room, sending more plaster raining down on our heads and shattering the fragile façade of calm I've acquired. Terror fills my stomach with shards of glass, and fresh adrenaline saturates my veins as the overhead lights flicker several times before winking out completely, leaving us in darkness, with only sounds of muffled gunfire overhead.

Nikolai. Alexei.

No. Fuck, no. I can't think about either of them getting hurt right now. Or Pavel or any of our guards. I have to concentrate on what I can control. I turn, groping my way through the darkness toward where I last saw the others when Chloe's tense voice reaches me.

"Slava? Slava, where are you? Alina, Lyudmila, you there? Where is he? I can't find Slava."

The shards of glass expand to fill my chest. "He was right next to you." I switch to Russian and raise my voice. "Slava! Slavochka, where are you?"

No answer.

Chloe's panic bleeds into her voice. "Slava! This isn't a game. We're not playing hide-and-seek. Lyudmila, do you see him?"

Lyudmila answers in her ungrammatical English, sounding just as worried. "No. Maybe he hurt. I search now for light."

Yes, flashlights. Good idea. I grope my way toward the drawers in the back, where they're supposed to be, when I hear Chloe call out, "Slava? Slava, come here!"

Did she find him? I turn and blink at the faint light coming from the other side of the room. Chloe is already heading for it, shouting Slava's name, and to my horror, I realize where the light is coming from.

The ladder leading up to the garage.

The ceiling hatch must be propped open.

Chloe is already scrambling up the ladder. I run after her. "Chloe, wait!"

Lyudmila materializes in front of me, blocking my way just as a sharp, acrid smell reaches my nostrils.

Smoke.

It's coming in from above.

Either the garage or the house is burning.

"Wait," Lyudmila hisses. "We need to—"

I shove her aside. "Let me through! Slava is—"

"We can't just run out there!" She grips my arm. "We need a plan."

I have a plan, but it's not one she's going to like. I'm shaking all over, my skin so icy it might as well be a winter day instead of an unseasonably warm September night. "Stay here," I say, my words tumbling over one another. "I know exactly what to do."

I twist out of her hold before she can reply and dash toward the ladder. The gun is still in my hand, its cold weight both sickening and reassuring. Gripping my long skirt in my free hand, I hike it up to my thighs and climb up the ladder, ignoring the way my high heels catch on each rung.

The higher up I go, the stronger the smell of smoke gets, and by the time I emerge into the garage, my eyes and throat burn. I drop to my knees and suck in a lungful of relatively clean air, then hold my breath as I stand up and take in the scene in front of me.

It's like something out of a war zone: smoke and flickering flames, cars covered with a white layer of broken plaster, their windows shattered by the force of the blast. The explosion tore a giant hole in the big metal door of the garage, leaving nothing but mangled edges and fire in its wake.

That fire provides enough illumination for me to see Chloe's white dress out on the driveway, her posture screaming of tension as she stops abruptly.

I duck down to suck in another semi-clean breath, and then I run after her, my heels crunching on broken glass and plaster. My throat burns, my eyes water, and my head throbs with agony, but I keep going, keep moving toward the scene that I know will devastate me —one way or another.

Time seems to slow, each step requiring an inordinate amount of effort, each second stretching out into an eternity as the deadly standoff out on the driveway comes into view.

My brother and Alexei, their guns aimed at each other.

And in the middle, Slava, his eyes wide with fear and incomprehension.

Something cold and clear inside my mind sifts through the implications. No gunfire is audible now, so Alexei's forces must've neutralized Nikolai's guards out on the perimeter of the compound. What about Pavel?

He's supposed to protect the house itself. Is he alive? *Please let him be alive.*

I lengthen my strides, but I might as well be moving through molasses. The entrance seems impossibly far as Chloe brings up her gun, pointing it at Alexei. "Drop your weapon and back away!" Her voice is a trembling, smoke-hoarsened croak.

No, foolish girl! He'll kill you! I want to scream the words at her, but my lungs are already howling with the need for air, and I need every bit of oxygen I have left to make it there and stop the nightmare that's about to unfold.

Alexei's gaze flicks toward her. *Don't. Please don't.* To my relief, he doesn't move. "Come here, Slavchik," he says in Russian. His deep, disconcertingly calm voice sends hot and cold chills down my spine. "Quickly."

My brother's snarled reply is in English. "My son isn't going anywhere with you. Slavochka, get behind me. Go now."

The words barely reach me over the roar of my heartbeat. The flames by the entrance are growing closer, dancing in my vision. Out on the driveway, my nephew is the very picture of confusion, his gaze bouncing between the two men he knows. "Uncle Lyosha? Papa?"

Like the brave idiot she is, Chloe edges forward. "Slavochka… Please come to me. Mama Chloe needs you here."

My nephew hesitates, as if he knows what will happen once he's no longer between the two lethally armed men, but then he makes his choice. As Chloe takes another cautious half-step forward, he dashes toward her, his short legs pumping hard, and she grabs him by the arm and shoves him behind her.

Rat-tat-tat!

I stumble and brace myself against a car as horror jellifies my legs and paints my vision gray. It takes me a second to realize that I imagined the explosion of gunfire, that everything on the driveway is still status quo.

I suck in a smoke-filled breath as my tortured lungs give out—only I'm close enough to the entrance that the air is breathable again. Pushing away from the car, I suppress a cough as I hear Alexei's rough bark of laughter.

"Mama Chloe, is it?" he drawls in English. The sound of his voice, dark and taunting, makes my knees go weak again. "Sweetheart… if you move another muscle, I'll blow your brains out and then your dear husband's. Congratulations on your nuptials by the way. I'm guessing the wedding was very recent?"

I'm still trying to get my legs to move when my brother replies in a lethally soft tone, "None of your fucking business. Now leave before I paint the ground with *your* brains. Since we seem to be family and all, I'll let you walk away before the guards get here."

"What guards?" Even through the smoke, I catch a flash of Alexei's white teeth as he bares them in a sharp, cruel smile. "It's just me and my men here now. And you're fucking high if you think I'm leaving without what I came for. Hand over my sister's son and Alina—and maybe, just maybe, I'll let you and your pretty bride live. Seeing as we're about to be even closer family and all."

My heart jolts sideways, and I almost miss my brother's next words, spoken in an even softer, smoother voice. "You have exactly thirty seconds to shut up and back away before I open fire."

Alexei's gaze flicks to Chloe again. "With her and the child here? I don't think so. Besides, my snipers have you both in their sights."

"Bullshit," my brother says coldly. "They don't have a clear shot."

Alexei's grin is pure savagery. "No? Want to bet? Either way, all I need to do is wait, and my men will take down the shooter on your roof—at which point you'll be completely surrounded, and I'll take what I came for."

Strength flows back into my legs. The shooter on the roof—that must be Pavel. He's still alive. I propel myself forward as Nikolai's voice becomes pure ice. "Not if you're dead by then. You have twenty seconds left. Nineteen. Eighteen…"

Alexei's eyes turn into slits, and I can read my brother's death in their black depths—and in Nikolai's tense stance, I can see Alexei's demise. Violence fills the air, its thick, noxious fumes as toxic as the smoke swirling around me.

It's now or never.

We're officially out of time.

I cover the last meter to burst into view. "Stop!" My eyes water from the smoke as I step through the jagged hole left by the explosion, my gun held loosely at my side and my gaze trained on the man I've been trying to escape for nearly half my life. "Stop, Alexei, please. Slava isn't going anywhere, you know that. My brother won't give up his son. And he's not—" My voice breaks as the full knowledge of what I'm doing slams into me. "He's not the one you want anyway."

At my side, Chloe sucks in an audible breath, but I ignore her, my eyes locked on Alexei's. His gaze scorches me in return, the dark hunger in it visible even from this distance. My heart hammers faster. Clad in black tactical gear, with the weapon in his hands, my nemesis looks as deadly as I know him to be, yet even now, some tiny part of me burns for him—and an even smaller part, one that I don't want to acknowledge, weeps in gratitude that he's alive.

"Alina, get back." My brother's voice is knife sharp, but I ignore him too. This is now between me and Alexei.

A numb sort of calm envelops me as I raise my gun, aiming it at him. My voice is level as I say, "You have a choice. I know you're an excellent shot, but so is my brother—and so am I. And so is Lyudmila in there." I nod toward the dark garage. I'm bluffing, but I can't let Alexei know that. With superhuman effort, I continue in the same even tone. "Maybe you can take down one or two of us before our bullets find you—and maybe your snipers can help—but nobody is going to walk away unscathed. You might have the advantage of the forces surrounding us, but here, we outnumber you. Besides…" I manage to inject sarcasm into my voice. "What good am I to you dead, right?"

"Alina, shut up and get back inside," Nikolai says harshly. "You don't have to—"

"I will come with you," I continue as if my brother hasn't spoken. "I will honor the betrothal contract. And in exchange, you will call off your men and forget all about my nephew. He belongs here, with his father and Chloe—you can see that for yourself."

Alexei's gaze strays toward Chloe for an eyeblink, taking in the sight of Slava clinging to her as she shields him with her petite body, looking as fierce as any mama bear. The child's eyes are wide and fearful; we've all been speaking English, so he wouldn't understand the specifics, but there's no mistaking the tension in our postures, nor the guns we're all pointing at each other.

If Alexei tries to take his nephew as well as me, blood *will* be spilled, and the irreparable trauma the child will suffer will be on his conscience.

Alexei's gaze returns to my face, and I shudder at the fury—and the burning hunger—in it. Yet his voice mirrors mine in its evenness. "All right. We have a deal. Lay down the gun and walk toward me."

"Do not fucking do it," Nikolai bites out. "I can take him."

"Maybe." My pulse pounds sickeningly in my temples as I lay my gun on the ground. "Or maybe you'll both die. Maybe Chloe and Slava will as well. Think about that."

Nikolai's voice is tense. "I'm not letting you do this."

The smile that springs to my lips coats my tongue with bitterness. "It's not your call, brother. Nor is it mine. That whole fate business you believe in? Well, mine was decided when I was fifteen, and it's time I stopped running from it. You and Konstantin have shielded me long enough."

Before he can argue further, I hurry over to Alexei —who grabs my elbow in a steel grip as soon as I'm within reach and pulls me against him, pinning me possessively to his side. Even with the smoke lingering in my nostrils, I can smell the wild forest essence of him, and my body vibrates at his proximity, my skin flashing cold and hot as I fight to subdue the complex mix of emotions that closeness to Alexei always generates.

After all this time, all these years, he's here.

He's come to claim me.

Deep down, I've always known he would.

Across the driveway, my brother's face twists with fury. He starts toward us, only to stop when Alexei's finger twitches warningly on the trigger.

"Don't, Kolya," I say hoarsely as Alexei begins dragging me toward the tree line, gun still trained on Nikolai. Each word is another nail in my coffin, but I push ahead, raising my voice as the distance between me and my brother grows. "I'll be fine. Just take care of Chloe and Slava, and I'll see you back in Moscow sometime, okay? And tell Konstantin not to look for me. I don't want blood spilled on my behalf!"

I shout the last words as the dark forest closes around us, leaving me at the mercy of my captor—the man I've just agreed to marry.

My worst nightmare come true.

Chapter 27

Present Day, Location Unknown

Opening the door to the cabin, Alexei shepherds me inside, his hand still on my elbow. In the two minutes it took us to walk down here, the storm arrived in earnest, the torrential rain lashing at the circular windows as lightning flashes twice in a row. Claps of thunder follow a second later, making me jump again even though I expected them—a sign of just how on edge I am.

This is it.

No more running, no more hiding, no more delays.

After more than a decade, my day of reckoning is at hand.

Alexei turns me to face him before letting go of my arm. With the sun hidden behind the thick clouds, the cabin is cloaked in shadows, the daylight filtering in through the windows too weak to dispel them. Too gray to chase away the darkness pressing in around me, or the fear twisting my insides and making my pulse race.

The fear *and* the desire.

I swallow hard and back away as another bolt of lightning illuminates the cabin for a moment, highlighting the sharp, taut lines of Alexei's face and the scorching hunger in his eyes.

"You have no idea how long I've wanted you," he says in a low, guttural voice as he reaches for the hem of his black T-shirt. With a swift, economical motion, he pulls the shirt over his head and lets it drop to the floor. His voice deepens into a rough growl. "How long I've waited for you."

All the saliva in my mouth evaporates as the cabin tilts around us, the yacht rocked by the ever-growing waves. "It's hardly waiting if you fuck other women." I think I sound coherent, but I can't be sure. My heart slams sideways against my ribs, and my skin burns as if I were in the grip of a fever. I've never seen Alexei shirtless, not even in the PI photos, and the powerful, starkly masculine lines of his torso exceed anything my imagination has conjured up over the years.

Thick, hard-muscled shoulders and strong, defined pecs taper in to a lean waist, with each ab muscle sharply delineated. Like his arms, his chest is decorated with tattoos that form a dark, intricate pattern on his tan skin. Crisp black hair swirls around his nipples and dusts the middle of his chest, and below, a thicker line of hair bisects his lower abdomen before disappearing into his low-riding jeans.

I've never thought of Alexei Leonov as beautiful, but he is. Terrible and beautiful, like some artist's depiction of a demon.

His ab muscles ripple as he gives a short, harsh laugh. "You think I've been fucking other women?"

I force my gaze up to his face. "Haven't you?"

The expression on his hard features makes my breath catch. "No, my beauty. From the moment our betrothal contract was signed, I haven't so much as kissed another woman."

I swallow, instinctively backing away again, and he comes after me, each stride a predator's deadly prowl. My pulse leaps higher as the backs of my knees touch the bed and he looms over me.

He grips my cheeks, pouting my lips, and leans in, onyx eyes burning into me. "I wanted to." His voice is a harsh, dark rasp. "Believe me, I fucking wanted to. So many times, I wanted to forget you, to walk away and find someone else… anyone else. But there's no one else for me. I've known it from the moment I saw you in that hallway outside your father's office, back when you were still a fucking child… a child dressed up and painted to look like an adult."

He pushes me down onto the bed, and I'm so stunned that I don't put up a fight as he covers me with his large, hard body, pinning me in place. Holding himself up on one elbow, he twines the other hand in my hair. His gaze burns me alive as he continues thickly. "I thought you were eighteen—seventeen, at worst—but you weren't even fourteen.

And I fucking wanted you. Do you know what that made me?"

I blink up at him, my hands gripping the sheets on either side of me. "I…"

"A pervert. A pedophile no better than that fucking tutor of yours."

My breath seizes. "Is that why you killed him?"

"He touched you." Rage ignites in his eyes and reverberates through his voice. "I saw him touch you. All those months, I fought to forget you, telling myself that you were way too young, that it was unforgiveable to want you, and there he was, lusting after you with no trace of shame. Touching you like it was his right."

I somehow find a shred of sarcasm. "When it should've been *your* right?"

"Exactly." His eyes gleam in the shadowed interior of the cabin as his voice turns dangerously silky. "That's when I knew I had to arrange our betrothal."

His words stun me all over again, to the point that it takes me a second to find my tongue. "You… *You* arranged it? Not our fathers? But—"

"Oh, they believed it was their idea." A flash of lightning illuminates his sharp-edged smile. "Your father, in particular, was convinced that it was all his doing… that he was manipulating my family into doing what he wanted." He loosens his grip on my hair before moving his hand to cup my jaw. A rolling boom of thunder shakes the room, and when it fades, he continues, the tenderness of his touch a stark contrast to the darkness of his words. "The betrothal was the best way to ensure that you'd be mine when you grew up, that no other man but me would ever have you. The alternative—stealing you from your family and keeping you locked up until you were old enough—was going to be my plan B, but luckily for you, I didn't have to implement it." His mouth twists. "Or maybe unluckily. I still regret that I didn't take you away the day you turned eighteen."

My lungs contract with every word he speaks until my breaths are so shallow I can't draw in enough air. It's as if the storm outside is sucking all the oxygen from the cabin, the gusting wind penetrating through the windows and bringing in a chill that invades my entire body, freezing me from within.

Alexei arranged our betrothal.

It wasn't some business arrangement that he reluctantly accepted because I was pretty. It was something he'd wanted from the start—something he'd orchestrated. After the fiasco of my eighteenth-birthday party, I knew he desired me and intended to go through with the marriage, but I still thought he was just making the best of a bad situation. I ascribed his stalking of me to lust mixed with some perverse desire to adhere to his father's wishes, but that wasn't it at all.

When I was just a child, he'd decided he wanted me, and he tied my life to his with a ruthlessness that would do Machiavelli proud—a ruthlessness that's all the more terrifying given that he'd been only nineteen years old himself.

If he could do that then, what is he capable of now that he's thirty?

How far will he go to ensure that I remain his?

As if reading my thoughts, Alexei shifts his lower body to lie directly over mine. Something hard presses against my thigh, spiking my pulse and kindling a familiar flame in my core, a heat that chases away some of the chill inside me. "I have you now," he whispers roughly, stroking his thumb over my cheek. "I have you, and I won't let you go. So you might as well come to terms with it, Alinyonok. You can fight if you want, but it won't do any good."

No, it won't. Another flash of lightning lights up the room, revealing the volcanic heat in his dark eyes, the merciless intent in the harsh set of his features. He's done being patient. Eleven years ago, he chose this fate for us, for me, and there's no escaping it.

"I hate you," I whisper, staring up at him. My eyes and throat burn with unshed tears, but I force the words out because they're the only weapon I have left. "For the betrothal and for everything you've done since, I will *always* hate you."

His face tightens, as if from a physical blow, but then he smiles again and it's a cruel, dark smile. "So be it. For the rest of today, though, you're going to love me."

And shifting his hand to encircle my throat, he crushes his lips against mine.

Chapter 28

Present Day, Location Unknown

Is it love if it's not your choice?

Is it force if you embrace it?

One day, I will think about that. One day, I will figure out the answers.

That day is not today.

As the storm rages outside, the waves rocking the yacht from side to side, the only thing I'm aware of is the growing maelstrom inside me, the way Alexei's kiss sucks me into a vortex of raw, carnal need.

Gripping my throat with one hand, he explores my mouth with the same ruthlessness he's applied to capturing me. His tongue sweeps deep, and I catch a faint hint of champagne on his breath, taste his victory over me as my body ignites with familiar fire. Instinctively, I lift my hands to clutch at the hard muscles of his shoulders. His bare skin is hot and smooth under my palms, and I find myself running my hands down his powerful arms, his sides, his back, seeking more as I helplessly return the kiss.

His hold on my throat isn't tight enough to restrict my breath, but my head still spins from lack of oxygen as he settles more firmly over me, the hard, heavy weight of him preventing my lungs from dragging in enough air. Or maybe he's just stealing all my air with his kiss, like the demon that he is. Either way, I feel like I'm caught in a dark dream, an erotic nightmare in which my body refuses to do my bidding.

I should be fighting. I should be clawing and kicking to get away, but instead, I feverishly arch into him, my thighs parting to cradle the hard bulge in his jeans against the part of me that throbs and pulses with a desperate need for him.

A low growl rumbles in his throat, and he tears his lips away, breathing heavily. Staring down at me with burning onyx eyes, he shifts his weight to lean on the elbow of the hand that's gripping my throat and hooks his other hand into the bodice of my dress. Roughly, he yanks on it, ripping the expensive fabric along with my bra to bare my breasts to his gaze.

When his eyes meet mine again, they're so ravenous I quake inside.

"You…" His voice is low and hoarse. "You, Alinyonok, are everything."

Not giving me a chance to respond, he bends his head and closes his lips around my left nipple. His mouth is soft and wet, his breath scalding hot, and as his cheeks hollow with suction, I feel an answering pull deep in my core. I gasp from the force of it, from the sudden coiling of erotic tension, and he repeats the action with my other nipple before hooking his hands into the torn edges of my dress and ripping it further, baring my quivering stomach to his devouring lips and tongue.

Fuck. Fuck. Fuck.

I squeeze my eyes shut and bury my fingers in his hair as he trails his open mouth down my body, ripping apart what remains of my dress along the way. I know where he's going and I know I should stop him, but I can't. I simply can't. Every cell in my body is on edge, every muscle so taut it's trembling. Waves of heat radiate outward from my core as he circles my navel with his tongue, then moves lower, lower… Oh, God. I clench my fists in his hair as he rips away my thong, and his hot breath washes over my tender flesh before his lips press against my sex.

He feasts on me with soft, gentle nibbles, using his lips more than his tongue, and it's so much more than I imagined, the sensations shocking and exquisitely acute. He's only exploring my outer folds, not the throbbing bundle of nerves inside, but I feel each kiss, each lick, each gentle grazing of his teeth as if he were doing it directly on my clit. Pleasure, sweet and sharp, pulses through me, adding to the tension, and it's both too much and not enough.

"Please…" I arch my hips, needing more. Seeking more. "Alexei, please…"

He ignores me. Pinning my straining thighs with

his strong hands, he continues his tender torment of my flesh, the oh-so-light kisses and nibbles that are driving me insane. I'm panting now, my nails digging into his scalp, but he proceeds with his maddening agenda and the tension grows until I'm vibrating with it, until incoherent moans and pleas escape my throat. Only then does he part my folds with his tongue, and finally, finally, he presses his mouth where I need it most—directly over my aching, throbbing clit.

I gasp, straining upward against his hold as the pleasure spikes unbearably, bordering on pain. His tongue is soft and wet, dangerously skilled. I'm excruciatingly close to the peak, and he keeps me there, balanced on the razor-sharp edge between agony and ecstasy. I'm going to die. He's going to kill me, I can feel it. I'm burning, sweating, trembling, my heart pounding so hard it's bound to explode, and then he slides a finger inside me, pushing it deep into my soaked channel, curving it in that way he's done before —and *I* explode.

I come so hard I see bolts of lightning behind my closed eyelids, and every nerve in my body quakes as wave after wave of ecstasy thunders over me, making my inner muscles spasm and turning my mind utterly and completely blank.

I'm still drifting in the pleasure-soaked aftermath when he moves up over me, covering me with his body once again. The orgasm was so intense I feel as if I've been drugged, and my lids weigh a kilo each as I pry them open to stare up into his face. His jaw is taut, his forehead dappled with tiny beads of sweat as he settles over me and gathers my wrists in one strong hand to pin them above my head. His expression is implacable, determined, and a prickle of unease penetrates the sensual fog encasing me as, with growing clarity, I recall the stinging pain when he broke my hymen with his fingers.

"Alexei…" I wet my lips, my heartbeat picking up pace at the memory of the massive pressure of his cock starting to push inside me before my bodyguards burst in. "Alexei, I…"

He kisses me. It's a sweet, tender kiss, nothing like the way he devoured me earlier. I can taste myself on his lips, and the reminder of what he did to me and the incredible pleasure I experienced rekindles the heat inside me, easing the gathering tension in my muscles. His lips are soft on mine, the strokes of his tongue gentle and soothing, and I find myself melting against him despite my fear… even as I feel the smooth, broad tip of his cock pushing at my entrance.

It's as big as I recall from our last close encounter, but it doesn't hurt this time, at least not at first. It starts off as an unfamiliar stretching pressure, my body's natural lubrication easing the way. But then… Oh, God, then the stretch increases, and it begins to sting as my flesh resists further penetration. I tense, my breath catching, and try to twist away from his kiss, but he grips my jaw with his free hand and forces me to face him.

Breathing raggedly, I meet his gaze as a blinding

flash of light outside illuminates the cabin, followed by a boom of thunder. The rain is now a constant drumbeat, nearly drowning out the pounding of my pulse. With my wrists confined in his grasp above my head, my dress torn in half, and his cock buried partially inside me, I've never felt more vulnerable, more helpless. More at his mercy.

His chest moves with heavy breaths as well, his jaw tight with the strain of holding back, of not thrusting as every male instinct undoubtedly demands. A bead of sweat rolls down the side of his face as he says hoarsely, "Alinyonok… I don't want to hurt you, but—"

"Liar," I whisper on a shaky exhale. Of course he wants to hurt me. How could he not? For running away, for disappearing, for rejecting him throughout all these years, he can't not want to hurt me, to punish me, at least a little.

His eyes flare, and I know I'm right. Consciously or not, he doesn't just want to possess me—he wants to make me pay. And on some level, I want that too. Because I deserve it. Because I need it.

If I'd been less of a coward, we could've been here years ago, without all the suffering, all the deaths.

With our eyes locked, I see the exact moment his iron self-control shatters. A shudder ripples through his powerful body, and with a guttural growl, he surges into me, penetrating me all the way in one brutal thrust. The shock of it reverberates through my body, making my breath seize and my muscles go rigid. It's more than a stretch, this merciless invasion, and the tears I've been holding back leak out of the corners of my eyes as I writhe against him, my inner tissues struggling to adjust to his immense size. The pain kills the last remnants of the heat inside me, leaving behind only a cold, bitter sense of violation—and it's a victory of sorts.

The last thing I want is to enjoy this.

Only... he manages to stop, teeth gritted as he holds himself still, his cock lodged deep inside me. His gaze homes in on the wetness on my temples, and he swears, squeezing his eyes shut. When he opens them, they blaze with grim determination. "No," he growls. "Nice try, but this isn't how it's going to go."

Keeping his hold on my wrists, he shifts his weight onto that elbow and wedges his free hand between our bodies, moving it down to where we're joined. Unerringly, he finds my clit and applies pressure, making my breath catch for a different reason. It's no longer pain that rockets through my nerve endings, making my inner muscles squeeze around his thick cock—nor is it precisely pleasure. But as he begins to move his fingers in tiny circles, I find my hips shimmying with the same rhythm, chasing more of that distracting sensation, that pressure that doesn't eliminate the painful fullness inside me but makes it tolerable. Makes it... oh, fuck.

I close my eyes, not wanting him to see the defeat in my gaze, but he knows anyway. He always knows. His lips ghost over my eyelashes, then over both of my temples, kissing away my tears, and his fingers pick up pace. With preternatural, demonic patience, he coaxes out my arousal, making my body soften against my will. Before long, the heat inside me returns, and so does the aching tension. I shouldn't be able to respond again, not with my body filled so ruthlessly, so fully, yet I can't help myself. My breath comes in panting gasps, my brain swimming with endorphins as I strain my arms in a futile effort to free my wrists, and the erotic tension grows, crowding out the pain, drowning out everything but the knowledge that I've lost this battle... that eventually, I'll also lose the war.

"Look at me," he orders hoarsely, and I have no choice but to comply.

Opening my eyes, I hold his gaze as he begins to move inside me, filling me with hard, driving thrusts, his face taut with the strain of controlling himself. Then that unnatural control of his cracks again, and he takes me with all the savagery he's kept so carefully leashed. Each brutal stroke of his cock fills me and destroys me, taking me ever higher until my vision glows white and my breath hisses between my clenched teeth. Until every muscle in my body spasms and releases as I scream his name, while he groans and thrusts even deeper before shuddering over me in his own powerful release.

Until there's no doubt that he's won, and I'm now his.

Chapter 29

Present Day, Location Unknown

The storm has passed, the waves lapping gently at the hull by the time Alexei carries me into the adjoining bathroom. Through the circular window by the tub, I catch a glimpse of the clear night sky speckled with stars before he flicks on the light switch with his elbow, flooding the room with brighter light.

Somebody must've drawn a bath for us earlier because the clawfoot tub is full. By now, however, that water must be cold. Alexei must reach the same conclusion because he carries me straight into the shower stall, where he carefully sets me on my feet and turns on the water.

I shiver at the initial coolness of the spray and back away, only to give a start when the cold tiles press against my shoulder blades. I lean back against the wall anyway, my legs too weak to support my weight. Biting my lip, I close my eyes and try to steady my breath, ignoring the throbbing soreness deep inside me.

Three times. That's how many times he's taken me today, wringing pleasure from my sore, exhausted body and giving me only a few minutes of respite in between. I guess I shouldn't be surprised. If he's told me the truth about not fucking other women since our betrothal, he has a decade of sexual deprivation to make up for.

I still don't know if I believe it. Or maybe I don't want to believe it. Because the implications of that are as terrifying as the knowledge that he's been behind this nightmare of a betrothal all along. That he's been the puppet master, not a fellow puppet as I'd imagined.

"Here, it's warm now." His touch pulls me out of my thoughts, and I open my eyes as he maneuvers me under the spray, which is now at the perfect temperature.

I blink, wiping the water off my face with both hands, and he gives a low, delighted laugh, his dark eyes shining as he looks at me. And why not? I'm his favorite possession at the moment, the toy he's been after for so many years.

"So what's your plan?" I ask, because I have to. I do my best to keep my eyes on his face instead of his naked body, magnificent though it might be. I don't want him thinking I'm up for round four. "Are you going to keep me on this boat forever? Fuck me until I literally can't walk?"

He trails his gaze over my breasts, my stomach, the

apex of my sex, and when his eyes meet mine again, his smile is the darkest yet. "No, my beauty. Well, yes to the last one, but not the first. As fun as this vacation is, I'll need to return to Moscow after a while—and you will come with me when I do."

Though I know he's most likely toying with me, a spark of hope flickers to life. "Oh? When will we go?"

If he brings me back to Russia, my brothers will find me, no matter where he stashes me, no matter what I told Nikolai about not wanting them to look for me. They'll figure out a way to get me out, away from him, and maybe, just maybe—

He spreads his hand over my belly, his palm so large his fingertips touch both of my hipbones. "When you have given me a child to replace the one your family has stolen from us," he answers softly, his eyes gleaming like black jewels. "That's when I'll bring you back. That's when you will no longer want to run."

I go cold despite the warm water pouring over us. I'm not on the pill—I never had a reason to be—and now that I'm not so overwhelmed, I realize I didn't see or feel a condom during any of the three times he took me.

He's fucked me bareback, repeatedly, and he intends to do it again… until eventually, I fall pregnant. Until we're once more joined by blood, only through *our* child—an infinitely stronger bond.

"No," I whisper, staring up at him as tears of despair flood my eyes anew. "No, please, Alexei… don't."

He cups my jaw, tilting my face higher. "I have to,"

he says, sounding almost regretful, and presses his lips to mine, kissing me as tenderly as if he hasn't just blown up my world.

As if he hasn't plunged me deeper into my worst nightmare, extinguishing what little hope I had left.

Sneak Peeks

Thank you for following Alexei and Alina's journey! Their story continues in *Beautiful Chains*.

To be notified about my future books, sign up for my newsletter at www.annazaires.com.

Are you craving more dark, suspenseful romance? Check out my bestselling *Tormentor Mine* series, the thrilling story of a Russian assassin bent on revenge and the woman he becomes obsessed with.

Do you enjoy laugh-out-loud romantic comedy? My hubby and I cowrite raunchy, geeky romcoms under the pen name Misha Bell. Grab a copy of *Sextuplet and the City*, the super sweet story of a dessert-loving secret blogger, her sexy Latvian ballet dancer crush, and one night in Vegas that changes everything.

Are you an Urban Fantasy fan? Check out *Dream Walker*! Written by my hubby Dima Zales, this is a mind-bending tale of a dreamwalker on a mission to save her mom—without falling in love with the dangerous illusionist helping her.

If you like audiobooks, please visit www.annazaires.com to check out this series and our other books in audio.

Now, please turn the page to read excerpts from *Tormentor Mine* and *Sextuplet and the City*.

Excerpt from Tormentor Mine by Anna Zaires

He came to me in the night, a cruel, darkly handsome stranger from the most dangerous corners of Russia. He tormented me and destroyed me, ripping apart my world in his quest for vengeance.

Now he's back, but he's no longer after my secrets.

The man who stars in my nightmares wants me.

"Are you going to kill me?"

She's trying—and failing—to keep her voice steady. Still, I admire her attempt at composure. I approached her in public to make her feel safer, but she's too smart to fall for that. If they've told her anything about my background, she must realize I can snap her neck faster than she can scream for help.

"No," I answer, leaning closer as a louder song comes on. "I'm not going to kill you."

"Then what do you want from me?"

She's shaking in my hold, and something about that both intrigues and disturbs me. I don't want her to be afraid of me, but at the same time, I like having her at my mercy. Her fear calls to the predator within me, turning my desire for her into something darker.

She's captured prey, soft and sweet and mine to devour.

Bending my head, I bury my nose in her fragrant hair and murmur into her ear, "Meet me at the Starbucks near your house at noon tomorrow, and we'll talk there. I'll tell you whatever you want to know."

I pull back, and she stares at me, her eyes huge in her pale face. I know what she's thinking, so I lean in again, dipping my head so my mouth is next to her ear.

"If you contact the FBI, they'll try to hide you from me. Just like they tried to hide your husband and the others on my list. They'll uproot you, take you away from your parents and your career, and it will all be for nothing. I'll find you, no matter where you go, Sara... no matter what they do to keep you from me." My lips brush against the rim of her ear, and I feel her breath hitch. "Alternatively, they might want to use you as bait. If that's the case—if they set a trap for me—I'll know, and our next meeting won't be over coffee."

She shudders, and I drag in a deep breath, inhaling her delicate scent one last time before releasing her.

Stepping back, I melt into the crowd and message Anton to get the crew into positions.

I have to make sure she gets home safe and sound, unmolested by anyone but me.

Order your copy of *Tormentor Mine* today at www.annazaires.com!

Excerpt from Sextuplet and the City by Misha Bell

What happens in Vegas stays in Vegas. Or does it?

Okay, let me explain. I broke into my crush's dressing room to sniff his tights (not in a pervy way, I swear!) and got busted while, um... you get the idea. He then kind of, sort of blackmailed me into agreeing to a fake green card marriage with him. But hey, I'm not complaining.

Next thing I know, we're on a flight to Vegas to make our friends and family think we had a crazy drunken night and, in the spur of the moment, tied the knot. Except... that's exactly what happens. (Thanks a lot, vodka.)

Considering that he's the most desirable ballet dancer in New York City and I'm a garage-dwelling secret blogger with a major sweet tooth, there's no way this marriage could ever become real. Not to mention my totally crazy family and my aversion to every smell under the sun—except his.

All I can hope for is to not fall in love with my husband. That shouldn't be too hard, right?

Holy spirit and mother of all pheromones.

This was a huge mistake.

Musky and delicious in a manly way, this overwhelmingly arousing smell is doing the exact opposite of what I hoped and expected.

The Russian could bottle this aroma and make a fortune.

Damn it. Operation BS is a huge flop. Instead of getting him out of my mind, I've just wedged him in there so deeply it's a wonder my ears don't pop.

Oh, and that fetish I was claiming not to have—I might've just developed it, at least as far as this man's undies go.

Why me, universe? It's bad enough I can't be with a realistic prospect due to my heightened sense of smell. Why should a guy I can never have smell so heavenly?

I force myself to pull the dance belt away from my nose. Instantly, I miss the scent. Also—and this might be due to the orgasm interruptus during the performance—I'm hornier than a teen bonobo.

Hmm. I *am* wearing my sex toy underwear… And I do have this delicious thong at my mercy… Most importantly, life has just handed me a new lemon in the form of The Russian's god-like scent, so the least I can do is make sweet, orgasmic lemonade out of it—as per my motto.

Oh, and this could also be inspirational for my blog.

In fact, I owe it to myself and my followers to do this.

There. It's settled. Before I can chicken out, I lock the door, plop my butt on the chair, and turn on my vibrating panties.

Oh, wow.

This is amazing—and the only way I can make it better is by picturing The Russian's powerful legs, each muscle flexing as he leaps across the stage.

I gulp in another whiff of the aphrodisiac undies.

Fuck. This feels better than anything in recent memory, and not just thanks to the thong. It must be the naughtiness of the situation. After all, I *am* masturbating during a breaking-and-entering. No, make that spelunking during a robbery. Because who am I kidding? I'm stealing this dance belt after I'm done.

Unbidden, the image of The Russian's mouth on my clit comes to mind. He's pursing those uber-lickable lips and blowing a cherry to generate the sensation that matches the vibrations I'm feeling.

Ooh. Nice. I increase the speed of the vibration and close my eyes.

Yeah. Just like that.

Blow another cherry for me.

A little more.

Yes.

No.

Damn it.

For some reason, the orgasm is too far away, probably because the real Artjoms Skulme is only here in spirit, unlike during the performance.

I increase the speed some more.

The gizmo purrs louder and the orgasmic horizon moves close enough that I can't help but moan—but I do manage to keep my volume low in case some cleaning person happens to walk by the dressing room.

A minute later, the orgasm is still not coming.

I take another hit of the magic scent and picture The Russian's tongue flicking over my sex.

It's great, don't get me wrong, just not enough. I think what's keeping me from reaching my destination is this gnawing emptiness that I yearn to fill. More specifically, to fill it with Mr. Big, as that's what my nose has been smelling. Unfortunately, the closest I can get at the moment is my fingers.

I let the remote join the thong in my left hand to free up my right digits. Pretending they're The Russian's, I lick and suck my index and middle finger, then slide my hand into my still-vibrating panties and locate my entrance.

Fuuuck.

This is exactly what the masturbation doctor ordered. Now that the feeling of fullness is there, the orgasm rushes forth at the speed of sound.

Also, the images. Oh, the images… The Russian is pounding into me, hard, his pelvis performing tricks that only a ballet dancer is capable of.

Another moan escapes my lips, one that might be a tad too loud. Oops. I muffle the next moan with the dance belt.

Wait a sec.

Did I just hear a clack?

Nah. Must be my jaw clicking from holding in a scream.

I'm almost there. Just a few seconds more. I take a deep whiff of the thong, inhaling the arousing aroma like I'm underwater and it's my oxygen.

I'm almost there.

So close.

Just a little bit more—

Now the sound is unmistakable.

The hinges on the dressing room door squeak.

My eyes fly open.

Before I can remove my fingers from inside myself and create some distance between the dance belt and my nose, a man steps into the dressing room.

A man who's starred in all of my recent fantasies.

The Russian himself.

Order your copy of *Sextuplet and the City* today at www.mishabell.com!

About the Author

Anna Zaires is a *New York Times, USA Today,* and #1 international bestselling author of sci-fi romance and contemporary dark erotic romance. She fell in love with books at the age of five, when her grandmother taught her to read. Since then, she has always lived partially in a fantasy world where the only limits were those of her imagination. Currently residing in Florida, Anna is happily married to Dima Zales (a science fiction and fantasy author) and closely collaborates with him on all their works.

To learn more, please visit www.annazaires.com.

Made in the USA
Middletown, DE
20 September 2023